SerpentineS

ISBN: 0-6157-2207-5
ISBN-13: 9780615722078

SerpentineS

Giuseppe Savino

Publisher
2012

Chapters

Preface

It was a good life. Noah Blakely was one of those fortunate people we all know: he had a bright future ahead, he had recently graduated from law school, he was married to a smart beautiful woman, and he was the father of a healthy, happy daughter.

Life and fate took him on a roller-coaster ride, giving him all he wished for, only to take it away, but allowing him to keep what he really cared for, deep in his soul.

"SerpentineS" refer to the curved shape of an object or a design that resembles the letter s, a sine wave, or a snake; the latter is a derivation of the term. This book takes its name after serpentines, for their shape can resemble the twists and turns of one's life. The word "serpentines" itself carries opposing meanings. It may symbolize the joy of a celebration or the evil associated with a snake. All these elements are present in the plot of the story you are about to read.

Sometimes fate turns lives around, twisting their paths randomly. We like to believe we make our own choices, and maybe we do, but who really knows? Life can be complicated as it is, but living a parallel one, even though amusing at times, may become a lot of work.

In its own twisted way, fate may even have its particular sense of fairness, and even when we don't really understand it at the very moment events happen, they may all be part of a larger picture that in the end balances out evenly.

A Graceful Decision

It was the last sip of the last glass of the last bottle. A fine Golden Gris wine, her favorite for the past years. This noble drink had been not only good company through the ups and downs of her now strained marriage but also a silent listener to her thoughts, questions, and wishes.

The fall had come early this year, almost as if it too wanted this tumultuous summer to be over. The leaves were starting to turn, decorating the landscape. The cold, dry wind of the season came and went, hovering wobbling between past and future. There were vestiges of the warmth left behind but also the fresh aroma of a new beginning, a new life.

She no longer knew the man who used to be the perfect husband. The last year had come with surprise after surprise, none of them good. There was something he was hiding, and it was impossible to figure out. She even confronted him about a possible affair, but after so long...it must be a relationship.

Maybe it was the brandy-fortified wine, maybe it was the fact she drank the full bottle, maybe it was the accumulated stress of the past year while watching her promising marriage fall through the drain, or maybe it was the combination of all these, but she had made up her mind: she was walking out the door to never return. Her baggage was light, at least the one that was visible. She only took a couple of suitcases, her daughter's favorite's toy, and her jewelry—all except for the wedding ring. The engraved words—Grace and Noah Forever—made no sense anymore. She left that inside the empty glass of wine on top of the nightstand on her side of the bed.

She knew more tears would come, but at least the agony of figuring out what was going on would end. Memories of better times crossed her mind as she loaded the car.

Because her father had passed away when Grace was only four, her mother had raised her. Grace had always wished to have a father for her daughter, but she also knew she could raise her daughter on her own.

Dreams had become unrealizable fantasies, and she would rather shoot for a fresh start. Dropping everything and moving on felt selfish at some level, but she justified it by thinking that Madelyn, her six-year-old daughter, deserved a better future.

The garage door closed behind them as she drove silently with tears in her eyes. The car moved slowly down the street, as if it had not decided its final destination. The trees waved their branches as the house looked smaller and smaller in the rear-view mirror.

A couple of years back everything seemed so different...

It was a life full of promises and promises full of life.

Two Years Ago

Noah and Madelyn were playing in the front yard. It was a Saturday morning in a quiet Midwestern suburb near Minneapolis. The winter was yielding to the verdant spring air wafting its way up from the Gulf of Mexico. The dryness of winter had receded, and the snow-covered ground absorbed the already quiet sounds of the neighborhood. The wind carried promise and anticipation in a way that only people living in northern latitudes can fully appreciate.

"Hey, Daddy, catch me," Madelyn yelled, as she ran back and forth teasing her dad. Noah played along and was enjoying every second of Madelyn's laughter.

"Can you help me climb the tree?" Madelyn pointed at the tall tree in the front yard.

"Sure, just be careful. The branches might not be very flexible, so stay close to the trunk," said Noah, as he lifted Madelyn to the first reachable branch of the tree. Madelyn grabbed it and started playing on the branch under the watchful eye of her dad.

Noah's phone buzzed, indicating an incoming text message. As he read it, his eyes became wider and wider. He ran into the house while screaming at the top of his lungs, "Honey, I got the job!"

"Honey, I got the job!" He kept on yelling as he climbed the stairs looking for his wife, Grace.

Grace stepped out of the shower, trying to figure out the reason for the screaming and sudden disturbance of the peaceful morning.

"What?" she asked.

"Honey," Noah repeated more calmly, "the job at Watson & Corcoran, remember I had applied for it? I really wanted this job. I got it! I got it!"

"That's great," Grace responded, trying to share the excitement. She was confused by all the sudden excitement and yelling going on. Noah's big smile indicated good news, but she was not fully following the situation. Something interrupted her thoughts. "Wait, where is Madelyn?" she asked.

"Oh, my God!" Noah said, "I left her in the front yard."

Grace rushed downstairs, an anxious mother searching for an abandoned child in the snow.

"Madelyn, where are you?" Grace yelled, panicking because she couldn't see her daughter.

"Up here, mom," Madelyn responded in a joyful tone.

"What are you doing up there? How did you get up there? Noah, come quick! Help Madelyn out of the tree."

Noah was just coming out of the house and helped Madelyn climb down from the tree.

Grace had a look of absolute disapproval on her face. "How could you leave her alone outside? And hanging abandoned in a tree!" Grace said, as she completely turned off the excitement of the moment.

Noah apologized and pointed out that nothing had happened to Madelyn. Grace tried to disguise her anger, tried not to spoil Noah's good news. She knew very well that after a few months without a job, this was indeed great news, but how could he abandon a kid in a tree?

"Honey, I'm sorry. This is great news, and I just wanted to share it with you," Noah said, looking for forgiveness. "Everybody wants to work at Watson & Corcoran, and now I'm in. It's an associate lawyer position, but I will escalate as fast as I can, and you know it," he continued.

"We have to celebrate," Noah announced, still immersed in his enthusiasm.

Grace gently left her state of anger at Noah for abandoning Madelyn in the tree. She understood that the news was quite important and that Noah's enthusiasm might have impaired his judgment for a few minutes. "I'll make a delicious dinner tonight," she said with the best possible smile she could offer, as she headed to the kitchen to evaluate what she needed to grocery shop for.

"Forget about dining in," Noah said. "We're going out. We have to celebrate big. I'll make reservations at La Belle Vie, and we'll invite some of our friends to come with. This is just great!"

"But, honey," Grace said calmly, "La Belle Vie is really expensive, and we can't afford it right now…"

"But we will!" Noah interrupted confidently.

Grace reluctantly accepted what she considered an irresponsible expense. In her mind, they shouldn't spend money they didn't have yet. She was aiming for an intimate celebration, but she understood Noah wanted to show off a little with his friends. Grace was also feeling a little guilty for spoiling Noah's fun. She didn't want to be upset about him leaving Madelyn in the tree. After all, nothing really happened.

She was no longer a fan of large groups and celebrations. Before having Madelyn, she used to lead large fundraising events for the arts, but she had grown accustomed to a much quieter family life, almost resembling what she had had as a kid.

Noah and Grace hired a babysitter and headed off to the restaurant. Dinner was great, and Noah spent most of the night relating future plans about how he would conquer higher positions in the firm and how good life would be. Grace was used to Noah's egocentric speeches and had learned to enjoy them.

They even ran into a couple of acquaintances whom they hadn't seen in years. Noah broke the news to them while taking some time to decorate the news with a description of the nice possibilities ahead.

Noah's job started a week from that Monday, so he spent the week shopping for new suits and reviewing some material to be up to date and well prepared. Grace had fun shopping with her husband. They had started dating many years ago, when Grace was just beginning her degree in liberal arts. By now, she knew how to handle all his tantrums about suits being out of date or not meeting his style.

It was a fun week. She was happy to see him so excited after a few months of watching him worry so much about the future. She knew how bright he was and had full confidence that he would do well at the new job.

The First Day

The first day at work is similar to your first day anywhere, from preschool to high school to college. You get to know your playground (classroom, office, et cetera), the different facilities (from bathrooms to meeting rooms), and your mates. In addition, you get to know the ground rules (both written and unwritten).

Noah shared the orientation day with another new associate, Joshua. Both Noah and Joshua were very smart guys. They flew through orientation, eager to start their jobs, but the last five minutes of their day set the tone for the next year.

Watson & Corcoran was very clear on the main goals. Mrs. Watson, one of the senior partners and evidently the one who called the shots, gave them some general guidelines about the rules of the firm. "Gentlemen, we are looking for one exceptional lawyer who we can present to our board as our new junior partner. There is only room for one, and the ideal candidate is one of you two. We will evaluate your performance, and by the fall of next year one of you will get the promotion. The other one will have to wait for another year and compete with the next candidate (or candidates)." Her tone was formal, direct, and authoritarian.

"At Watson & Corcoran, it is as important to have a great professional performance as it is to have a strong interpersonal role in the office. We pride ourselves on forming integral human beings who are also exceptional lawyers," she continued.

The message was clear. It was either he or Joshua who would get the upcoming promotion to junior partner at Watson & Corcoran. Noah was confident that after winning this first battle, the path toward senior partner shouldn't be that com-plicated.

Get Set...Go!

The first few weeks at his job flew by really fast. Noah was a talented person and was becoming very well regarded by the partners, but Joshua was a tough competitor. He was also well prepared and equally hungry for the promotion.

Joshua and Noah had become close colleagues, but they certainly kept an eye on each other. Noah had established good relationships with most of his coworkers.

One day at lunch, when he was short of cash, his colleague Wendy said she would take care of the check. But the conversation that followed added some stress to Noah.

"Thanks, Wendy, I'll buy next time. Even better, we will go to a much nicer place on my dime as soon as I get my promotion," Noah said with his very confident tone.

Wendy Thil had been an associate lawyer for years and knew the firm pretty well. She gave Noah a kind and condescending look, with a tilted head and a kind smile.

"Buy me lunch tomorrow, and we're even," she said with a smirk. "I'm not one who bets on lost causes," she continued.

"What?" Noah asked impatiently.

"Nothing," Wendy responded.

"Please tell me," Noah insisted.

"Well, let me put it to you in simple terms," Wendy said. "I like you, and I think you have terrific talent, but if I were you, I wouldn't hold my hopes up on the promotion. Have you done your homework? Do you know who Joshua Swartsman is?" Wendy spoke with a very smooth voice. It wasn't a whisper, yet it was not loud enough for someone to comfortably hear from a distance. It almost invited you to lean toward her to fully understand the message.

"I'm afraid you know something I don't," Noah replied intrigued.

"Joshua Swartsman is the nephew of Jacob Adler, senior partner at Watson & Corcoran," Wendy continued. "Noah, you are serving a purpose here. Your purpose is to justify before the board the promotion of Joshua Swartsman.

"The firm has two smart guys competing against each other, and when the time comes, they'll give the promotion to Joshua. He would not be appointed; he would have just won fair and square a competition against another lawyer: you."

"This is impossible," argued Noah in disbelief.

"Why? Would it be because we lawyers would never do something like this?" Wendy responded sarcastically. Her green eyes, almost hidden behind her red hair, looked directly into Noah's. "Look, I don't like this more than you do, but I've been here long enough to know how it works," She continued in her soft voice.

Noah went home that day fully aware of his clear disadvantage. He knew he had to overcome it and that talent alone would not get him the promotion.

Now he understood that while he had a good relationship with his co-workers, Joshua spent his time talking with the board members. They already knew about him. This was so not fair!

The Bike

Noah spent a nice weekend with Grace and Madelyn. They hardly spoke about the job. It was a very intense week for Noah, and all he wanted was a true break from it all.

Instead, they bought a bike for Madelyn. She picked a pink one with whitewall tires.

"Why does it have those tires in the back?" Madelyn asked.

"They are training wheels, honey," Grace responded.

"Well, I want that bike but without the wheels," Madelyn said as she pointed at the training wheels.

Madelyn was determined and fearless. Noah could see traces of his character in her, and that really pleased him. He asked the salesperson to remove the training wheels and bought the bike. Grace was a bit concerned about the wheels, but she bought the helmet along with all the protective gear so she could please both Noah and Madelyn.

Later that afternoon all three went to the park and started the biking experience. Grace and Noah took turns running by Madelyn while teaching her how to ride.

It was Noah's turn to run while stabilizing the bike from the seat. His phone rang. He let go of the seat and checked the phone. It was Joshua calling. Madelyn lost focus and fell a few feet away at the same time that Noah was using his best corporate greeting.

"Good afternoon, Joshua," he said, while ignoring Madelyn's crying.

Grace was carefully watching and ran to the scene to help Madelyn.

"Thanks, Joshua, I'll ask Grace, my wife, to check our agenda and see if we can join you guys. Can't promise you anything on such short notice," he continued on the phone while covering the microphone to ignore the chaos in the background.

"What were you thinking?" yelled Grace as she ran past him to help Madelyn.

"OK. Joshua, thanks for the invitation, will call you back in a few. Thanks again. Bye." Noah ended his phone conversation as he walked toward Madelyn.

Grace looked at him with disapproval and in disbelief.

Madelyn was OK, just a bit shocked.

"Why was it so important to pick up the phone?" Grace asked clearly upset.

"It was Joshua from work, inviting us for dinner tonight," responded Noah.

"How could you leave Madelyn alone? I don't care who calls! And by the way, I am not in the mood to see anyone tonight," Grace said. She was very upset since the same thing had happened a while ago.

While Noah requested more support from Grace in his career, Grace demanded that he be more attentive to Madelyn. Their discussion continued for a while; it was loud and public. This was the first time that they had had this kind of an argument.

Grace had been silently putting up with Noah's career becoming a priority over everything else. She could take a back seat herself, but when it came to Madelyn, she was not going to allow it.

Needless to say, there was no dinner with Joshua that night. Noah returned the call and presenting a compelling argument to justify their absence. It really bothered him. He needed to keep Joshua close since the competition for the promotion was really tough.

Noah knew he had messed up with Madelyn. He had never seen Grace so upset. It wasn't a good time to pursue the social gathering. He needed to find another opportunity to secure his promotion.

The rest of the weekend was uneventful and mostly quiet. Only Madelyn broke the silence once in a while, asking her parents to look at her recently acquired biking skills. They were far from perfect, but she was determined, just like her dad. Once in a while, especially when turning, she had to put her foot on the ground, but she was learning fast!

Monday was just around the corner, and it offered a much-needed tension breaker. Grace was looking forward to being a mom, and Noah was eager to resume his quest for the promotion.

First Attempt

Monday mornings were slow at Watson & Corcoran. Noah had not stopped planning how could he approach the board members and make them notice him.

He brought a box of chocolates to their administrative assistant. It was a failed attempt. Helga had no expression on her face and apparently no feelings or sweet spots to tap into.

"Leave them in the inbox; I'll open them at the end of the day. I appreciate your unnecessary gesture," she said, without even cracking a smile or taking her eyes away from the computer screen.

Noah returned to his office with a frustrated look in his face. He crossed paths with Joshua in the hallway and apologized once again for declining the dinner invitation.

"No sweat, we'll do it another time," Joshua responded with a wide smile. The guy was actually nice, but Noah felt that he had an unfair advantage.

Noah slowed down his pace, wondering what Joshua was doing, and more importantly, where he was going.

"Happy Monday!" Noah overheard Joshua greeting Helga.

"Good morning," she replied, expressionless.

"Is my uncle in?"

"Sure, do you want me to announce you?"

"Not necessary, thanks. Oh," he paused, "Who brought you chocolates?"

Helga didn't respond to that, but it was almost obvious. Noah had just been there, and this was an obvious and desperate attempt to get access to the board.

Later at lunch that day Noah casually approached the center table at the cafeteria. Most of the partners were sitting there, and the conversation was loud, accompanied by laughter.

"Good afternoon," Noah said with a wide smile.

"Good afternoon," some of them responded. But the conversation pretty much dried up right there. There was an uncomfortable silence with the look from some of the partners indicating, "So what do you want?"

"I have a few comments on the Jones case," Noah continued. He wanted to give them the impression that work was always on his mind. Plus, he also wanted to fill in the silence and give a purpose to the interruption.

"I am sure you are on top of it, but if it's anything urgent, just book a time with me later today," Jacob Adler responded.

"OK, sir," Noah said as he was backing up from the table nervously. Normally he was extremely confident, but approaching the partners under disadvantaged circumstances made him lose his focus.

He sat at the much less desirable table with Wendy. Wendy couldn't disguise her crooked smile.

"What?" Noah asked, with a bit of aggressiveness in his voice.

"Hey," Wendy protested. "Don't show me all those 'manly' gestures, right after you come here with your tail between your legs. Why do you want to complicate your life so much? I am giving you the script of the movie. Be patient. Let Joshua get the first promotion, and you'll get the next one when it becomes available. Heck, Joshua himself might be on your side."

The mere thought of being under Joshua in the firm hierarchy sent shivers down Noah's spine.

"How come you're not in the race?" Noah asked Wendy.

"Because I have other priorities," she said. "This is my job, not my life. I am a perfectly happy mother of two kids. They are my life. I come here and do my job, but my life's fulfillment comes from elsewhere. You instead want this to be your career, your life. Nothing wrong with it; I am just giving you the perspective of someone who has been here longer and understands how things work."

Wendy's words were in his head all that week. Noah even focused on buying a nice present for Grace. Her birthday was coming up on Saturday.

For a while, Noah was himself. He bought a nice bracelet and worked with the jeweler on the setting, so he could surprise Grace with it—as he had always done. He knew Grace was upset about the events on the previous weekend, so he wanted to redeem himself on her birthday weekend.

The Birthday Celebration

Saturday would be too obvious for a surprise, so Noah decided to give Grace her gift on Friday. He texted her from work: "Hi. Dinner with Joshua tonight at the St. Paul Grill; can you make it?"

"Sure, I guess it was bound to happen," Grace texted back.

"Perfect. See you there at six o'clock? Going straight from work."

"OK. I'll drop Madelyn at my parents' house."

That week, Noah had taken his focus off of his career and focused on Grace. He had the bracelet engraved, "Grace and Madelyn are my life."

Grace showed up at 6:00 p.m. sharp. She was always on time. The waiter guided her to a table at the center of the restaurant. It was set for four, as expected. Even though she was a beautiful lady and had no critical role in what she believed tonight's business dinner would be, she had spent time making herself look even better. She had a nice new black dress and a very simple and elegant pearl necklace that went perfectly with it. She wore high-heeled, brand-new shoes that matched her small purse. She liked to dress up, but in addition, she would not want to be outshone by Joshua's wife.

"No one else has arrived?" she asked the waiter.

"Not yet, Ms. Blakely," the waiter responded politely.

It wasn't a good feeling to be the first one and to be sitting right at the middle of the restaurant. She was used to Noah's company when they went out.

She texted Noah, "I am already here. How much longer? My parents were busy so dropped Madelyn at your parents. Too short of a notice to get a sitter!"

"On our way. Two more coming," Noah responded.

"Who? I need names."

No reply.

"Ms. Blakely," the waiter said. "We need to move you to this table. The reservation is now for a couple more people."

Now she was moving to a table by the window. With all the commotion in a quiet St. Paul restaurant, everyone had now noticed her presence.

It was now 6:30 p.m. Grace was getting impatient, but she understood that on a Friday, at the end of a busy workday, it was hard for people to be on time.

"Can I have a glass of white wine?" she asked the waiter.

"Sure, any preference?"

"Golden Gris," she responded quickly.

At 6:40 p.m., the waiter delivered her glass of white wine and an envelope. "This is for you, Ms. Blakely."

"What? From whom?" she asked. But the waiter had already left.

She opened the envelope and read the note inside. "Thanks for coming. You are the most wonderful person in the world. Love, Noah."

She smiled as she read the note.

When she lifted her eyes, there was a huge bouquet on the table.

She hadn't even noticed when it had been placed there.

There was a card on it with her name on it.

She opened the card and read it.

"Happy Birthday! With all my love, Noah."

Grace was pleased with the surprise, but this was not appropriate for a business meeting.

She was still dealing with the bouquet surprise when she heard guitars playing at the other end of the restaurant. She recognized the song; it had played on her honeymoon. She looked at the musicians, a trio, approaching her table. In less than two minutes, they had surrounded her while playing and singing. The song brought back great memories of the trip Noah and she had taken to the Caribbean.

Only when the song was about to end did Noah approach the table. He was holding Madelyn. Madelyn was all dressed up; she had a red bow on her light blond hair, matching the red case for the bracelet.

"Mommy, Mommy, this is for you," Madelyn said, as she handed Grace the bracelet case.

Grace, wiping her tears away, ran to hug Noah.

Her parents and Noah's parents were also joining the celebration.

Noah was relieved. All had gone according to plan. The only "random" aspect, the only place where things could have gone wrong, was where Grace would drop off Madelyn. It could have been her parents, his parents, or a sitter. Noah thought Grace would ask her parents, but since they said they were going to be busy, she opted for Noah's parents. This just added people to the celebration.

Grace was happy and surprised. She knew why she had fallen in love with Noah, and as she read the inscription in the bracelet she hugged him tightly.

"So there is no Joshua? No business meeting?" she asked.

"Nope," Noah responded. "It was just a cover-up to keep you from figuring out my plan."

The Next Big Idea

It was the beginning of another week. Noah prepared his next case. He was really good at it. Wendy gave him grief, as usual.

"You are working too hard," she said.

At lunchtime, Noah saw the partners' table from a distance. This time, instead of forcing a conversation, he just slowed down his pace as he passed the partners' table. He barely overheard them talking about their last boat outing.

Noah continued with a slow pace toward the usual table. Wendy was sitting there, fully aware of Noah's newest desperate attempt.

"Hi, how-are-you?" She said, talking to him really slowly. "Is-the-slow-mo-tion-only-for-walk-ing?" she teased.

Noah blushed.

"I am so glad you went to law school," she continued, "because you suck as a spy. What are you trying to find out?"

"I don't know. Anything, I guess," Noah whispered in desperation.

"And what did you learn?" Wendy responded, sarcastically. She had fun teasing Noah about his ineffective attempts at closing the gap with the partners.

"Nothing, they were talking about a boat outing."

"Oh, yeah," Wendy said. "Early this spring Mr. Koslow bought a sailboat, and he's got them all riled up about sailing."

"Does he know how to sail?"

"I don't know, and I don't care, but maybe you can use that question as an icebreaker next time you force yourself into their lunch group."

Noah smiled as he dismissed the remark. However, without knowing so, Wendy had sparked the beginning of a new plan.

On Thursday of that week Watson & Corcoran was offering a celebration dinner. It happened every year around this time, and it was supposed to be a motivational outing for the team. Senior partners would mingle with the "common mortals" of the firm and listen (or at least pretend to listen) to what they wanted to say.

Noah saw this as another chance to narrow the gap and get some extra visibility with the partners.

The firm reserved an entire section at The Dakota Jazz Club. That night after work, Noah and Wendy headed to the restaurant. Wendy, as usual, was hitting Noah with sarcastic remarks about his failed attempts to achieve the impossible.

As they approached the restaurant they saw Joshua walking a few steps ahead. He was as pleasant as always, greeting the owner and the waiters and engaging in fun conversation. They directed him to the reserved tables.

Adler, Koslow, and Corcoran were sitting together at a table for four. Joshua's first stop was at that table—once again, a few steps ahead of Noah. The partners offered Joshua the empty seat since Ms. Watson, the other partner, had been unable to make it to the dinner. Joshua accepted, indicating how honored he was.

Before taking the seat, Joshua gave Noah a quick glance of victory, with a brief smile. He waited, standing up by his prime seat as if he were guarding a treasure, just so he could politely—and very loudly—greet Noah.

"Noah! There he is—and with Wendy, of course. So great you two could make it."

It looked like just a polite and effusive greeting, but it was a loaded comment. Somehow Joshua was pointing out the close friendship between Wendy and Noah, leaving it up for everyone else to interpret if there was something else going on. It was not what he said; it was the tone he used that made more than one head turn around.

Watson & Corcoran was very conservative and had a pristine image in the community. It also had a strict policy prohibiting office romances.

Joshua was really good at using any opportunity in his favor. He had his uncle on the board, and now he had compromised publicly the relationship between Noah and Wendy. Joshua knew these two had become friends and understood how much Wendy knew about the firm, so he needed to throw a wrench into this relationship.

Both Wendy and Noah felt the punch. Even though nothing was going on between them, they instinctively moved a few inches away and greeted Joshua and the partners with a wide smile.

Noah and Wendy continued to mingle with the other "common mortals," but they kept away from each other all night.

Later on, after dinner, the partners led a motivational toast and started mingling with the rest of the staff.

"Mr. Koslow," Noah called from a few feet away. "Can I ask you a question?"

"You already did," Mr. Koslow responded with a smile.

Noah smiled as he approached Mr. Koslow. "I have a question about a boat I am looking at buying and thought you could give me some insights," Noah responded.

This was confident Noah talking. For some reason he was not feeling threatened by Mr. Koslow now. It could have been that Joshua was not around or that the topic was not work-related, but this time it felt like two guys talking.

"What kind of boat are you buying?" Mr. Koslow asked.

Noah couldn't believe it. Mr. Koslow had fallen for it. Now they had a topic in common. They were about to become "boating buddies." The ice was broken.

The only problem was that Noah had no intention (or money) to buy any kind of boat.

"Well, Mr. Koslow, the one on the top of my list is a thirty-two-foot Crownline."

Noah had been on a friend's boat just like that a couple of times. He remembered the boat's size and model; he was a master at using information.

"Where are you planning on keeping it, on the river?" Mr. Koslow was really interested in the conversation, but now Noah had to be quick on his feet and make up a story as the questions came. Better yet, he would have to remember it later. He purposely had selected a motorboat instead of a sailboat so he wouldn't be asked to sail.

"On Lake Superior," Noah responded. "My wife's family has a place close to Bayfield, Wisconsin." Bayfield was ideal. It was a four- to five- hour drive from Minneapolis, far enough to avoid any unplanned trips but close enough to justify having a boat there. Grace's parents did have a small cabin up there, except it wasn't on Lake Superior.

"Well, Mr. Blakely, I would suggest you go with a thirty-five-foot or larger boat for two reasons." Mr. Koslow was always very organized, even in conversation. "First and foremost, you don't want to tackle the Lake Superior waters with anything too small for it. Those waves can intimidate even large ships. Second, if you are already planning on spending a few bucks on a toy, don't be shy or cheap when it comes to the little details. You only live once."

"Thanks, Mr. Koslow, I'll keep that in mind," Noah responded with a wide smile, as Mr. Koslow slowly turned and returned to mingling.

Noah looked for Wendy. He wanted to tell her all about it. He found her across the room and approached her with a big smile.

"Wendy, I have to talk to you. Did you see me talking to Mr. Koslow?"

"Not now, Noah," she interrupted.

"We were discussing boats," Noah continued, oblivious to her comment.

"I said not now," she responded vehemently. Her voice was quiet, but her eyes were threatening. Then she slowly walked away.

Wendy

The next morning on his way to work, Noah called Wendy on her cell phone. Wendy refused to expand about the previous night's conversation. She suggested meeting at a coffee shop about five miles away from work.

Noah was certainly intrigued. He got there before Wendy and had her favorite twenty-ounce coffee waiting for her.

"Grande Skinny Latte for you," Noah greeted her with a smile.

"Good morning," she said. Her face was showing unequivocal stress. "Thanks for the coffee, but we have to keep our distance now inside or out the office," she continued in a monologue before Noah could even interject a word. "Listen, Noah, you're a great guy, and I know it. You are smart and a great lawyer. Now, if you want to fight the odds and continue this pointless competition against the nephew of one of the board members, a man who is as smart and as a good lawyer as you are, well, I applaud you for it, but you are in it alone. I am a mother of two, head of household, and I have enough going on in my life to add to it the stress of fighting an office gossip and potentially losing my job. I know the Joshua type. To be honest, it's not very different from your type. You guys will stop at nothing to get to the next level, and then the next one, and so on."

"Wow, he really got you with that comment," Noah joked.

"This isn't funny, at least not for me," Wendy continued. "Believe it or not, it's harder for a woman to find a job in this economy. I have mine. I like it. It allows me to live my life, and I love my life. We are friends, Noah, so please, stay away from me. I don't want to be a casualty in this battle. Do you understand?"

"Yes," Noah responded, a bit upset.

He was not only losing a friend. He was also losing a valuable ally. She did know a lot about the firm. Joshua had hit him hard with just a quick comment.

Things were going to be weird at the office. Noah had grown to be accustomed even to Wendy's sarcastic comments. The boat idea came out of one of them.

"Can I at least tell you about my conversation with Mr. Koslow?" Noah asked, by way of a peace offering.

"Noah, when I tell you I don't want to be involved, I mean I really want to know nothing about it," Wendy responded, leaving no room for doubt. There was no sarcasm, wit, or charm in her answer.

This time Noah realized once and for all that Wendy had her priorities well defined. She probably could have been as good a candidate for the promotion as he was; she just opted not to compete. She really wanted to add no complications to her life. Joshua's comment had turned Noah into a complication, and Wendy couldn't run away fast enough from him.

Weekend at the Cabin

"Have you decided on a boat?" Mr. Koslow interrupted the silence at Noah's office. "Don't wait for the summer to end."

"How are you enjoying yours?" Noah responded.

For the next half hour they engaged in boat talk, just as Noah had anticipated. They even had lunch a couple of times that week. Sure, this wasn't as strong of a bond as uncle and nephew, but it was progress.

Noah's plan was working. He needed to solidify it before moving on to the next target.

Later that afternoon, Noah picked up the phone and called Grace. He asked her help to plan a Fourth of July weekend at her parents' cabin. Grace was excited. This meant quality time with her husband and daughter. She jumped on the idea and started executing the plan.

They had a nice family ride up to Bayfield. Noah's job had taken so much of his time that family outings had become a rarity.

The cabin was a simple house surrounded by acres of trees that sheltered it from the wind. It was so peaceful. It was really like taking a break from the world. Surrounding the house was deck with some old recliners and rustic tables. Time really slowed down at the cabin. Spotty cell phone coverage and the lack of the Internet isolated them even more.

Early in the morning, after a peaceful night, Noah jumped out of bed and headed to town. Madelyn and Grace were still sleeping. Noah went straight to the marina. He had some old friends there.

It was good to see them after so long. It amazed Noah how nothing seemed to change with the passage of time in the town. Everybody was happy and cheerful.

Tyler was the one running the marina. He was a stoic Norwegian guy who had sailed Lake Superior countless times in all kind of ships.

"So Tyler, are there any boats for rent?"

"I am afraid not. Why do you ask?"

"Just planning an outing with the family."

"What kind of boat are you looking for?"

"A thirty-five-foot one, hopefully a Crownline."

"Wow, that's really specific; any particular reason?"

"I may be buying one soon, so I want to check it out first."

"Let me make some calls. There might be one for sale, and the owner might agree on renting it out for a day for a test drive."

"I appreciate that, thanks. Leave me a message on my phone. There is no reception in the cabin, but while in town I'll be able to pick it up."

Noah returned to the cabin for a nice home-made breakfast and a fun morning with Grace and Madelyn. It felt so good to take a break from the daily routine.

For lunch, the family decided to take a ferry trip to Apostle Islands. An old ferry departed hourly from Bayfield, taking people (and, if they wanted, their cars) for a twenty-minute ride to Madelyn Island. Madelyn was thrilled to have an island named after her.

Noah and Grace stood on the deck. The scenery was just breathtaking. As the ferry slowly departed from the mainland, the town of Bayfield decorated the background, making it look like a postcard. Century-old houses were surrounded by dark-green foliage, and steep streets faced the deep blue waters of Lake Superior. The cool breeze coming from the lake tamed the heat of the summer. It was just perfect.

Noah's phone rang. He stepped as far as he could from the ferry's engine.

It was Tyler. There was a thirty-two-foot Crownline for sale at a broker nearby. He could have the boat at his marina ready to go in a couple of hours. Noah agreed to rent it for the remainder of the weekend.

"Who was it?" Grace asked.

"I have a surprise for you," Noah responded while picking up Madelyn. "How do you feel about spending the rest of the weekend on a nice boat?"

"What? Which boat?"

"I rented one. I thought it might be fun."

"Sounds great!"

"Good! We'll pick it up after lunch at Tyler's marina."

Overall, it was a fun weekend. Noah insisted on taking hundreds of pictures of the family on the boat. He knew he was going to put them on his desk, and that would help his efforts to bond with Mr. Koslow.

He felt he was a genius. Not only he was spending quality time with his family, he was also gathering strong material to strengthen his connection with one of the board members.

Mr. Adler was going to support his nephew, no matter what, but Koslow might be inclined toward him. Now he needed to focus on the other two: Mr. Corcoran and Ms. Watson.

Flying Forward

Noah framed the pictures of the family enjoying the boat ride. He placed them strategically on top of his desk. They were supposed to spark conversations about his brand-new boat. As he was carefully setting them on his desk, Wendy walked in.

"Good morning," Noah said, happy to see her swinging by like old times. Except this time she was not smiling. She did not show any intention to share a coffee or a conversation.

"Mr. Corcoran got his pilot's license a few months ago," she whispered, while looking at Noah without blinking.

Noah didn't blink either. They had an unspoken conversation. Wendy was passing on critical information to Noah as she had done before but wanted to remain distant. She looked at the pictures for a second and looked back at Noah.

"Nice work," she said, still without blinking.

Her wide-open green eyes were full of words, but her lips didn't smile. She said nothing more and left Noah's office.

"It's amazing how on top of things this woman is," Noah thought. "She knows what I am doing without even talking to me. It's great to have her as a silent ally. On the other hand;—a pilot? Why can't these people choose normal hobbies such as golf or football?"

Noah knew exactly what to do next. He started to study flying jargon. Every night, right after dinner with his family, he would immerse himself in textbooks on flying. He had no intention of taking flying lessons, just as he had no intention of buying a luxury boat, but this was his modus operandi to build a communication bridge with Mr. Corcoran.

A few weeks later he was ready. He was delivering a presentation during a staff meeting. One of his strengths was to own the floor when he spoke. Both Joshua and Noah were very professional when delivering a presentation, but while Joshua was normally very serious, Noah had the spark and wit to crack a joke or two and really captivate the audience.

He opened by saying, "Since we don't want this case to go Tango Uniform, I present my apologies for an early departure. There is a No Joy witness and that I spotted when I check six to confirm it's not a bogey. I will be sure to provide an update when RTB."[1]

1
Bogey   An aircraft that is unidentified. The aircraft must be identified by some means,

visual or electronic, before action can be taken. See Bandit, Hostile.

Check Six

A reminder to look behind you. In an aircraft, twelve o'clock is directly in front of you, three o'clock is on your right, nine o'clock is on your left, and six o'clock is directly behind you. Often used as parting words (the equivalent of "good luck" or as a "watch your back").

No Joy

Failure to make visual sighting; or inability to establish radio communications.

RTB

"Return to Base." Radio call indicating aircraft is beginning journey home.

Tango Uniform

Phonetic pronunciation of "T.U." Literally, "tits up." Something that is "Tango Uniform" is dead, inoperative, broken, or otherwise malfunctioning.

There was silence on the room and he waited for a few seconds to read their faces. Wendy didn't know what Noah was talking about, but she knew what he was doing. Only Mr. Corcoran found some humor in Noah's words. He had read the message loud and clear. He didn't mention a thing, but the expression on his face showed he had enjoyed it.

"OK," Noah continued, "for you non-pilots, here is the close caption of what I just said. Since we don't want to fail in this case, I will have to leave the meeting early. There is a witness who has not responded to my calls. I found out about this guy when looking at some background material in the case, and I want to be sure that we get to him before the other party does. I will be sure to provide an update when I return."

And with that, Noah left, chasing after his witness.

Joshua was growing extremely nervous with all the rapport that Noah generated. Even his uncle was smiling.

"Why are you smiling?" Joshua asked his uncle in whispering frustration.

"It's refreshing," Mr. Adler responded.

Joshua slammed his hand on the table and stormed out of the room.

Mr. Corcoran was a bit more reserved than Mr. Koslow. It was somewhat more complicated for Noah to achieve the same level of intimacy with Mr. Corcoran that he already shared with Mr. Koslow, but he had done it.

The gap with Mr. Corcoran was closed. Long hours after work learning about flight jargon and reading magazines about planes were starting to pay off. Now just a couple of pictures at a local small airport and that would close the deal for future conversations.

That weekend, Noah took Madelyn to the Flying Cloud airport. It's a small airport on the west side of Minneapolis. Madelyn enjoyed watching planes taking off and landing while Grace enjoyed some peace and quiet and alone time at the house.

After a small plane landed, he asked the pilot if he minded Madelyn peeking inside the plane. Minutes later Noah had a whole array of family pictures by the plane. It was a piece of cake.

Noah's Big Heart

There was a mischievous smile of satisfaction on Noah's face that Monday morning. He was re-arranging the framed diplomas and honorable mentions on his wall, adding pictures of his family at the airport and boating.

"You are lucky there is only one more partner to work on. Otherwise you'd need a larger office." Wendy interrupted Noah's quiet celebration.

Wendy's voice startled Noah. There was so much he wanted to tell her, but she just wasn't available for conversation. Noah's mouth was open, ready to enunciate the first word, but Wendy's index finger went to her lips as an indication (more like an order) for him to be quiet.

"Ms. Watson loves charity," Wendy said.

And before Noah could even ask anything, Wendy took two steps backward and left his office.

This represented another challenge with a more complicated puzzle for Noah. Ms. Watson was about fifty-five years old and barely spoke to anyone who wasn't a customer or a partner. She was highly regarded by everyone in the team as a hard worker and as a good-hearted person, yet she was completely unapproachable. She had (or at least showed) no sense of humor or appreciation for it. Her communications through email or presentations at staff meetings were pretty much the same: short, concise, and with clear direction of next steps. Normally there were no questions asked. Rumor had it that even the other senior partners were in some fear of her. She might attack them in public or private should they try to cross her path.

Noah knew Wendy was not available to provide additional information. She had made it clear that she wanted no friendship with Noah, not even now when apparently the tables were turning in his favor.

For the following weeks, Noah devoted himself to his job and to keeping his relationships with Mr. Koslow and Mr. Corcoran going.

Back home things were going well with Grace. Noah dropped a couple of hints once in a while about his progress toward the next promotion, and that brought a sense of admiration and tranquility to Grace's life.

One night, while sorting through the junk snail mail, the next idea started taking shape. Grace showed Noah an invite from a local fundraiser. They were invited to a dinner party, and the restaurant would be donating the profits toward single mothers in need.

"So where exactly are the funds going to?" Noah asked.

"Not really sure. There's a website address on the bottom. Why?" Grace responded.

"Did you check it out?"

"Not really, but if you're curious I'll do so," Grace responded while logging in to the website.

Noah always considered Grace to be a very smart woman. She was intrigued by Noah's line of questioning, so she would focus on finding out more information about how the funds would be used.

Noah noticed that she logged in and read carefully the information on the site. She spent a few minutes looking at the different pictures and success stories posted there. Then she related the information to Noah, and soon they were off to their regular activities.

"Why were you so curious about the fundraiser?" Grace asked, intrigued.

"No reason in particular. I just wanted to know how the process worked," Noah responded, and he was not lying. What he omitted to say was which process he was observing.

The next morning he looked up some web developers on the Internet. He found a couple of freshmen studying computer science. Later that day they met at a coffee shop downtown.

"Hi, guys, I need your help. I need you to build a website for me. Nothing complicated. It would just have some stories, some pictures, and a few links. How much would it cost, and how long would it take you?" he asked.

The guys smiled. "How long would it take you to send us the pictures and the stories?" This was a piece of cake for them. They overcharged him a bit.

Noah offered them almost twice as much as they quoted. "I need this done as fast as possible. Can I count on you guys?"

"Sure, just send us the text and pictures and where you want the links to point."

During the next couple of days Noah wrote a few articles. The articles were thanking Noah Blakely for his immense contribution to:

The Bayfield's Women Foundation
An organization supporting
single mothers and battered women
in Bayfield County.

That weekend, Noah took his family on a quick trip to the cabin. It was the middle of November, so it was getting cold, but Grace always appreciated getting away from home and spending family time with her husband.

Grace made Noah's favorite meals. She packed the board games that Madelyn loved to play with her dad. Noah always had a great time at the cabin. His family was very important to him, and Grace was an amazing homemaker.

During the drive he asked Grace if she had packed his favorite sunglasses.

Grace gave a look meaning, "Are you really asking for that?"

"Is there anything wrong with the ones you are wearing?"

"It's just the glare of the road. It's distracting."

"You gotta be kidding me. Do you want me to drive?"

"No, I like to drive. It's OK." He sighed.

"OK, what's the big deal with the sunglasses?" Grace was getting upset. Didn't he realize how much work she had done putting the trip together? Was he really going to throw a tantrum over a favorite pair of sunglasses?

"Honey?" Noah asked, after about ten minutes of silence.

"What?" Grace responded, showing he was getting on her nerves.

"I think I remember where I left them."

"What? The glasses?"

"Yes."

"Where?"

"They are inside my red bag in the trunk."

"Well, good! The world is saved!" She couldn't believe they were still on the topic.

"Would you mind terribly bringing them to me? I'll pull over."

Grace looked at him in disbelief. He really wanted her to step out of the car on the highway at 30F to bring his stupid sunglasses?

But she didn't want to spoil the trip at its very beginning.

"Fine," she said, a bit loudly, and with a clearly upset tone. "Pull over."
Noah pulled over and opened the trunk.

Grace stepped out and shut the door, almost slamming it, and waking up Madelyn, who had been peacefully sleeping.

"What happened, Dad?" Madelyn asked.

"Shhhh," Noah indicated with a smile.

Grace opened the trunk and found the red bag. She unzipped it and found a dozen of her favorite scented candles, a bouquet with a card addressed to her, a few bottles of Golden Gris (her favorite wine), and the case with the sunglasses.

The card read, "For my Soul Mate. Thanks for making my life such a wonderful adventure. Love, Noah."

Now she was smiling. That was so typical Noah. How couldn't she have figured it out before?

She grabbed the case and brought it back inside the car.

"You are amazing," she said, and gave her husband a big kiss.

"Now, can I have my glasses?" Noah responded proudly.

"Sure," she said now, still smiling.

Grace opened the case, but instead of finding the sunglasses a beautiful necklace came out of it, surprising her. She was startled at first, but then she hugged Noah, while breaking up in tears.

He never ceased to surprise her. What a great man she had married.

The next morning, Noah took the family for lunch at their favorite restaurant in downtown Bayfield. It was still open, even though it was late fall and the tourists had all left. After lunch, they walked up and down the streets of the charming town. Grace still had a big smile on her face and was wearing her brand-new necklace. Madelyn was happy sharing time with her parents and posing for pictures. Noah was shooting pictures of the family and asking the nice locals to shoot pictures of them in every corner of the town: at the doors of city hall, by the churches, and with the lake in the background. Grace thought some of the locations were a bit strange, but she was too happy to even question that. She had a dream family—a healthy daughter and an amazing husband—and things were going well.

All she wanted to do was hold her husband's hand and enjoy every minute while watching Madelyn grow up. The crisp November air and charming images on every street in that small town made her want to freeze these moments forever.

The following week, Noah contacted the web developers again. He now had the pictures and the articles ready for the website. In his website, Bayfield had named him an honorary citizen and thanked him for his outstanding job helping out women in need. A few pictures accentuated the text.

One of the links on the website pointed to stories told by the women who this fundraising activity had helped. All of them had different stories, but they all thanked Noah Blakely for his generosity and hands-on collaboration in making their dreams a reality. Some articles even included thank-you notes from the kids telling their stories and describing Noah as a big-brother or father figure.

In another section of the website, authorities of the town praised the commitment and generosity of Mr. Noah Blakely. There was even a motion to name a street or a park after him.

The website was up and running in a couple of days. The domain name was BayfieldWisconsin.us, and it looked official. The guys did a great job.

Now Noah needed some old-fashioned advertising. He went to a printer to have some brochures done. Nothing fancy; they were just an invitation to one of Noah's fundraising events. They displayed some of the pictures from the website and some general information about Bayfield, and, of course, they clearly showed the website's address, www.BayfieldWisconsin.us.

The printer worked fast. In parallel, Noah was discreetly trying to force any kind of interaction with Ms. Watson. He had no success, and he backed up. Pushing too much could raise suspicion, so he kept on working on his relationships with Mr. Koslow and Mr. Corcoran.

Joshua and Noah joined forces on a few cases. Their relationship was cordial and professional. However, Joshua never insisted on inviting Noah and Grace again for dinner, nor did Noah ever invite Joshua and his wife.

Even though the official communication for the promotion was not until the week after Memorial Day weekend, the partners usually reached their decision sometime between January and March. It was November already, so the final day was around the corner. Neither Joshua nor Noah wanted to take unnecessary risks.

Noah was racking his brain trying to find a way for Ms. Watson to buy into his fake image of "community man" in Bayfield, but she wouldn't even acknowledge him. He had all the tools ready and had invested lots of time, money, and effort into it, and all were seemingly going to waste.

Finally he saw another chance. Mr. Koslow was sitting at a table, and Ms. Watson had just joined him for lunch. If he could just sit there for a couple of minutes, he would have a chance. He walked by very casually. He had come a long way since he had first tried that and Wendy had mocked him for his clearly fake approach.

"Mr. Koslow, Ms. Watson," he said, as he approached the table.

"Mr. Blakely," Koslow responded.

Ms. Watson only raised her eyes, and silently conveyed two messages. The first one acknowledged the greeting. The second one was, "Carry on; don't sit here."

Noah understood both of them.

"My apologies for the interruption," Noah said, looking at both of them. "I just need some procedure guidance. If I wanted to post these ads on the bulletin board, from whom should I get authorization?" Noah enunciated every word, but did not even pause to breathe. It was a one-shot chance.

"I don't think you can post anything on the board, but let me look at it, and I'll let you know during the day," Koslow responded.

"Thanks, Mr. Koslow." Noah left a few of them on the table and politely excused himself and left. He was positive that Mr. Koslow would not allow anything of a personal nature to be posted on the bulletin board. However, it was the only way so far in which the brochures and the website address would be in front of Ms. Watson's face.

Noah sat at a prudent distance but kept Koslow and Watson's table clearly in sight. For a full hour, just like a perfectly aimed TV ad, the brochure was in front of Ms. Watson. Toward the end of lunch, Koslow picked up the brochures, gave them a glance, and threw them in the recycle bin.

The waiting game had begun. Every half hour, Noah checked his site for traffic. Nothing happened for a few days. At the end of the fourth day, toward eight o'clock, just after dinner, Noah checked the site. Eureka! Ms. Watson had clicked on it from her work computer. She had spent about twenty minutes on it, enough to read most of its content.

Maybe Thanksgiving week had slowed down her workload. The reason was unclear, but she had checked it out. Every week, Noah would post a new story, a new picture, or a new article from the Bayfield authorities.

Christmas season was in full swing. Noah knew that Ms. Watson was checking his site often, yet her attitude toward him had not changed.

Then, just before Christmas, as he was walking out of the office for a week's vacation, he heard his name called.

"Noah," a voice said.

He froze and turned around slowly.

It was Ms. Watson. The same stone lady who had never even responded to his greetings was now calling him by name.

"Yes," Noah responded in a broken voice, almost in fear.

"I just want to wish you and your family a Merry Christmas," she said with a quarter of a smile.

"Thank you," Noah responded excitedly as he took a step toward her.

Her eyes were already focused down on the paperwork on her desk.

"You too," Noah said, trying to regain her attention, but it was too late. She was ignoring him and everybody else again.

Christmas Dinner

Questions started pouring into his head. Was this good or bad? He was eager to go home and check his computer for any reported new traffic from Watson. Noah slowly turned around and was startled by Wendy, who had quietly stepped out of her office.

She indicated with her index finger for him to follow her. There was a big smile on her face. Noah followed her into an office around the hallway.

"Way to go! I think you have her on your side too," she whispered while still smiling. "How did you do it? Wait, not here. Let's go out and have a drink to celebrate," she said, as she pressed her finger onto Noah's lips to keep him from talking.

They walked out the building and went into a bar a few blocks away.

"So now you're talking to me," Noah said.

"Take it as a Christmas gift," Wendy joked. "By the way, we have not spoken, but I have given you the most critical information for your endeavor; have I not?"

"Yes, you have," Noah conceded.

They ordered something quick to eat and a drink.

Noah felt great. He had missed Wendy's company. The talks with her had also inspired many of his ideas. She was fun, quick-witted, and absolutely tuned into what was going on at the firm.

"Hey, I got news for you," she said. "Now this is a bit of speculation, but I've noticed Joshua and Mr. Adler arguing more than normal lately. I would guess Joshua is feeling threatened by you."

"Really?" Noah smiled with satisfaction. The truth is he felt as threatened by Joshua as Joshua felt threatened by him.

"Yeah. I've heard great comments from Koslow and Corcoran about you. You certainly have them on your side, but today you got a Christmas greeting from Ms. Watson. Way to go! How did you do it? That's really hard."

Noah's ego was skyrocketing right now. "I couldn't have done it without the key information you threw at me at the right time," Noah responded, hanging on to the last reminiscence of humbleness he had.

"Please, I don't deserve any credit at all. You're the master. So I understand the boat strategy and the pilot classes, but how did you get Ms. Watson on your side?"

Noah just looked at her and smiled mischievously.

"That's not fair!" Wendy said with a flirty voice as she ordered a couple of martinis. "So I am always there watching out for you, providing you with the key information, and you won't even share your successes with me."

Noah held his ground pretty well, that is, until the third martini. He was happy and buzzed.

"OK, Wendy, I think you are a piece of shit for not talking to me over the past months."

"You are a big guy, and you'll get over it. So are you going to tell me your secret or continue to act like a little kid?"

The excessive alcohol in his blood, combined with the celebration of his success, had elevated Noah's ego, and he really wanted to boast about his triumph. Plus, there was Wendy: a mysterious person, sometimes warm, sometimes distant, but always sarcastic, humorous, and beautiful. Noah's elevated ego and Wendy's persistence in understanding how he had executed his plan made him tell her all the truth and nothing but the truth.

"OK. I'll let you in on the first little secret." Noah was having a hard time pronouncing his r's. The martini effect was affecting them.

"R-R-Re-Ready?"

Wendy rose her glass, indicating she was.

"There is no boat." Noah confessed.

"What?"

"Yeah, I made it up."

Both burst out laughing, and Wendy raised her glass once again in a sign of approval.

"Really? You had Koslow and the rest of the office completely fooled. Oh, my goodness, you are terrible!"

"That's not all," Noah added. His ego was way ahead of him, and he was thrilled to be impressing Wendy.

"Is there more?"

"Sure. I am not a pilot."

Another burst of laughter.

"I can't believe it. Seriously? You made it up? That deserves a double toast," Wendy said, while ordering yet another martini.

They kept on drinking, laughing, and mulling over the recent revelations.

"Wait, wait, wait a second," Wendy said again, with her right index finger up.

"So I assume all this crap about the charity work is fake too?"

"Triple toast!" Noah responded, finishing up his martini.

"Oh, my," Wendy said in disbelief. "How did you do that?"

"That was easy," Noah's ego responded. And he proceeded to give a detailed description of each and every one of the steps he had done to build his tailor-made persona.

Every word he said amazed Wendy even more. "You are a maniac," she exclaimed while having another sip of a brand-new martini. "Nope, you are not a maniac; you are a piece of shit. You are way smarter than anyone, including me, gives you credit for! Here, cheers for that!" she said, toasting with her martini. They laughed all night through every detail of Noah's stories, until the bar closed.

Neither of them could drive. They had had more than their share of martinis. The bar called them a couple of cabs and sent each of them home.

Grace wasn't thrilled at seeing Noah arriving home drunk—and in the wee hours of the morning. She didn't want to make a big deal about it, but of course there were enough grounds for a bit of a conversation the next morning.

"How are you feeling this morning?" Grace said quietly while bringing him a glass of cold orange juice.

"My head is about to explode," Noah responded quietly and slowly while grabbing the orange juice and finishing it almost in one sip.

"Do you feel like talking about it?"

"Sure, honey. I'm sorry. I had a bit too much to drink."

"With the guys from the office, I assume?"

"Nope, just Wendy," Noah responded.

"Just the two of you, and you got drunk?"

"Yeah."

"Something else you want to tell me?"

"Not really. Are you jealous?"

"Nope. Should I be?"

"I know how this may sound, but I want to assure you that there isn't and never will be anything going on between Wendy and me. We were sharing stories about work and drank a bit more than we should have. That's all," Noah reassured Grace.

This wasn't a typical Noah behavior, but she decided to take it easy, let it pass, and focus on the Christmas party planning.

'Tis the Season

It was a snowy winter. Even before Christmas Eve, snow was covering every inch of the city. It was a peaceful view. Regardless of what lay under the snow, it all looked smooth, white, and pure.

The fireplace kept the living room warm. Madelyn added some playfulness as she excitedly opened her presents. Santa was great that year; he had brought everything she asked for and more!

Noah opened the present that Grace gave him. He carefully unwrapped the neatly packed rectangular box. He had to smile when he saw the present and read the card.

It was a beautiful wristwatch, and the card read: "So you can see every minute that I am thinking about you. With love, Grace."

It was time for Noah's present. Grace was excited. He always managed to surprise her, but she thought she was getting better at figuring out what the surprise was. This time the box was the size of a shoebox, but she knew shoes wouldn't be a Christmas present from Noah.

She finished unwrapping it and saw a standard cardboard box. As she peeked inside, she saw a piggy bank and a card. It was the ugliest piggy bank anybody could imagine—smiley, white, and shiny, with golden lines decorating its contours. She went for the card, and it read: "So I can help you save for whatever you want. Merry Christmas."

This was disappointing. Really? A piggy bank? Bad thoughts crossed her mind. How could he do something like it? And the card? What kind of message did he want to deliver with this? Was this related to his late party with that Wendy woman from work?

"Do you like it?" Noah asked.

"Not really," she said.

"Well, I'll try to do better next Christmas," Noah responded, completely unaffected by Grace's reaction.

He turned the computer on and logged into his fake website to check on its traffic.

Grace's lower lip was shivering. How could you approach this situation? How could anyone explain such a radical change in behavior?

"Noah," she said. "Is there something you want to tell me?"

"Not really. I just wished you a Merry Christmas, honey."

That was it. She couldn't take it anymore; there was something wrong, and she wanted to find out. The box was lying on her lap with the smiley piggy bank looking at her. With an abrupt movement she put it aside so she could walk across the room and get Noah's attention.

As the box landed on the couch, Grace felt something move inside the piggy bank. She shook it and confirmed something was in it. The plug on the bottom was well sealed with a powerful adhesive. She shook it to confirm something was inside, and looked at Noah.

Noah was watching his computer screen, oblivious to the situation.

Grace had no regard for the ugly piggy bank, so she smashed it as a discreet outlet to her frustration. A small box and another card emerged from the inside. She picked up the card from the pieces and read it: "But perhaps I can save you some time (smiley face) Love, Noah."

The box contained a pair of diamond earrings. She had commented on a pair similar to them while watching the Oscar Awards a few months back. Despite the beauty of the earrings, the fact Noah that remembered and looked for them was really special. Once again, Noah had surprised her.

A New Year Full of Surprises

Every new year comes with new hopes, new goals, and resolutions. It wasn't any different for Noah. He was zeroed in on his promotion.

He arrived early for the first day of work of the year. Wendy was already there. They had not spoken since their night of sharing martinis.

"Happy New Year!" Noah said effusively as he stepped into her office.

"Happy New Year to you too," she responded very seriously, barely lifting her head. "How can I help you?"

"What?"

"Nothing has changed, Noah. We are not friends at the office; remember? Is there anything I can help you with?"

"Not really," Noah responded, frustrated and confused. He left Wendy's office. "What a weird woman," he thought.

The new year was picking up speed. Noah confirmed that Wendy's comments about Joshua and his uncle were true. It was common to see them arguing, although in quiet voices, with gestures indicating both were really upset.

The firm had landed a high-profile case. A Hispanic adult male had—allegedly—committed a minor robbery at a local retail store. The store had called the police. Minutes after, the police spotted the suspect, based on the description provided by the store manager. The suspect had tried to run away from the police. After a few blocks of hot pursuit, several police officers had tackled the suspect and arrested him for being in possession of the stolen merchandise. After the arrest, the suspect had been diagnosed with irreparable brain damage, due to contusions caused by repeated blows to the head with a blunt object. The suspect's family was now suing for police brutality.

It had been in the press for a while. Both sides had passionate supporters, and the media feasted on the public's strong opinions.

Watson & Corcoran decided to represent the Hispanic male, and that put them in the eye of the storm. Beyond the money involved, there were two other factors that made the case really important. The first one was that it was their very own Ms. Watson who had brought it to the firm. The second one was that winning it would significantly boost the firm's reputation, but losing it would have a devastating effect.

Noah was on the partners' good side. On the other hand, Joshua's erratic and borderline childish behavior had created some doubts in the partners' minds about assigning such a case to him. They felt that even as a second chair lawyer for this trial, Joshua represented a risk not worth running. The partners were also aware that the race for the promotion was too intense between Joshua and Noah. They felt the two young lawyers' need for recognition could work against the firm.

During the staff meeting, Ms. Watson announced that she was assigning Noah and Wendy to the case. She appointed Noah as the lead trial attorney and Wendy as second chair. Ms. Watson also set high expectations and presented the risks and rewards of winning or losing the case. However, she emphasized the risks more than the rewards. She wanted to be sure both Noah and Wendy understood how high the stakes were.

Joshua took this as a personal offense. Ms. Watson was basically taking him out of the game. All this built-up pressure started to show its ugly face.

"How come you're not assigning me to the case?" Joshua interrupted Ms. Watson's closing statement at the staff meeting.

The partners kept silent. Mr. Adler bowed his head almost in sign of shame. Even Joshua understood his indiscretion—after he spoke.

Ms. Watson paused and looked at Joshua for about ten seconds before pronouncing a word—ten uncomfortable seconds that felt like a week for the people at the table, and probably even longer for Joshua.

"I am equally or better qualified than those two." Joshua cracked under the pressure of the silence and the intense stare of Ms. Watson.

"Mr. Swartsman, I believe that while you may or may not have similar qualifications to successfully address this case, there is something that's bothering you so much that you appear unstable. This somehow impedes your ability to adequately handle high-pressure situations. This case, as I mentioned before, is a high-profile one with elevated stakes for the client and for the firm. It's in the best interest of the firm, and maybe even in yours, that you shouldn't be involved in it. Should you want to appeal my decision or to submit it to further discussion you are free to do so now, or you may book a time with me to discuss it in my office. Should you agree with my decision, however, we could all happily proceed with the meeting," Ms. Watson responded to Joshua, whose expression of repressed anger was like that of a five-year-old who has been told there is no ice cream for dessert.

Ms. Watson managed to deliver her response slowly, as if she were enjoying how each of those words would hit anyone who had questioned her decision without a valid reason. She also managed not to blink even once, which made her stare uncomfortable for Joshua and even for the other ones at the meeting who were not under her merciless fire. She paused for a few seconds and then aimed her eyes at Wendy and Noah.

"Ms. Thil, Mr. Blakely, I wish you the best in this case. You will have all the files and relevant material on your desks in a few hours. Please keep me posted of any progress," Ms. Watson said in a different tone.

"Any questions?" She took a few seconds to look around the table. She paused longer as she looked at Joshua. Nobody said a word.

Meeting adjourned.

Wendy and Noah worked together on the case, but all their conversations were strictly about the case. Noah cracked a joke or a funny remark once in a while, but Wendy ignored them and focused on the case.

A few weeks later Wendy and Noah were stunned by an email from Joshua. He had resigned. Knowing he had no chance for the promotion and having his pride hit by working on a lower-profile case than Noah was more than he could handle. He presented it as a chance of taking a rare opportunity for advancement in his career, but both Wendy and Noah knew the real reason.

"You know, probably Mr. Adler already knew Joshua wasn't going to get the promotion, so he gave Joshua the inside scoop," Noah whispered to Wendy across the table.

Wendy responded by handing Noah an article with information regarding a key witness in the case. "Would you like to look deeper into this?" she asked, while completely ignoring the previous remark.

Case Closed

Two and a half months of intense litigation and meticulous press scrutiny were exhausting. The shortest day included fourteen hours of intense work hours under excruciating pressure. Ms. Watson was following this case like a hawk and would question any setback. The press waited for them at every corner, looking for a chance to get a bit more of information about the case. They had to watch every word, the firm said, even if it wasn't directed to the press; any leakage or comment that could be misinterpreted could have serious consequences.

The last day of the trial arrived. Wendy had masterfully interrogated all witnesses. She was very methodical in her line of questioning, and little by little she consistently crushed each and every one of the defendants' arguments. There was hardly any doubt the accused was guilty, but the closing was coming, and she knew Noah was better at it than her.

She placed her hand on Noah's knee and leaned toward him. Noah leaned toward her.

"Closing time. This is your time to shine," she said. Her lips touched Noah's earlobe a few times while delivering the message. This took Noah by surprise. She had always been very good at keeping her distance. Her movements, just as her words, were carefully planned. Why had she done that? Was it just a mistake?

Noah was aroused and for a few seconds lost concentration. He had no interest in Wendy, but it was undeniable that she was a very attractive woman. Not only was she beautiful; she knew how to use her beauty. There was an air of mystery around her. The media had picked up on it and speculated about her private life. When the media asked her either about the case or her private life, she always responded elusively but with a slight and pleasant smile and a kind look from her wide green eyes.

"I wish I could tell you more, but this is a high-profile case, and it's in the best interest of everyone related to it to observe maximum discretion about; don't you think so?" she would respond to questions about the case. And all of a sudden she would be the one interviewing the media.

Then she would thank them for their time with a sweet and candid voice, fix her hair, and with a slight smile, exit the scene.

When asked about her personal life, she would immediately respond that she had the most normal and boring life, but then she would aggressively start questioning back. Generally she had done her homework and knew a few facts or gossip about the main journalists. She would use this to drill down on them and completely control the focus of the interview.

Noah had been by Wendy's side all along the trial, so it didn't take him more than a few seconds to regain control of the situation. He knew it was his time to shine. Even though he had barely spoken during the trial, he was fully aware of every detail about it.

Noah delivered a masterful combination of knowledge, skills, and theatrics. He emphasized key points, directing the jury's focus not only with words but also with matching body language.

The jury was fully engaged, showing signs of empathy with the message he was sending them. Some of them were even nodding favorably.

And just like that, in less than five minutes he had delivered a compelling closing. The courtroom was silent for a few seconds even after he was done; it was as if the judge was also immersed in Noah's closing.

Now all they could do was wait. Noah and Wendy went back to the office. Although it was April, the weather was unusually warm. There was no snow left on the ground, and spring almost felt like summer. It was good to feel the warm breeze on their faces.

They walked silently. The journalists followed them, yelling questions.

"What do you think the jury will decide?"

"Can you share your thoughts about the trial?"

"Is this your most important case?"

"Can you share how you did your research?"

"What are you doing next?"

Noah was expressionless; Wendy smiled.

There were so many people in front of them that they couldn't keep walking forward. Wendy paused as if she wanted to respond to some of the questions.

"We just finished a long trial, and very soon you will have every single detail," she said casually and very slowly, as she kept moving forward. She would stop talking every time someone would impede her next step forward or interrupt her with a different question. While stopping she would give a kind look but assign the blame for her silence to whomever had interrupted or blocked her progress. In a matter of seconds, the crowd was trained. They were shushing each other and leaving an ample pathway for Noah and her.

"As I was saying, we just finished a long trial and very soon…"

"Can you give us any details?" a journalist yelled.

"Shhhhh," the crowd yelled back.

"It's important for us," Wendy continued, "in a high-profile case like this one to deliver all communication in a crystal-clear way. We don't want, as I am sure you don't either, to generate any kind of confusion with incomplete or inaccurate statements. So it's as important for you as it is for us to allow us to respond in a timely and organized matter to your very valid questions. Do you agree?"

"Yes!" the crowd yelled. Some people were even taking notes.

Before the reporters in the crowd were able to articulate the next question, Wendy and Noah had arrived at the entrance of the building. They went right into the elevator.

Her smile switched off once they were in the elevator. Noah wanted to chat and made a couple of attempts, but Wendy was as cold as stone. The elevator door opened, and she headed to her office as if it were any other day.

Noah was puzzled. They had basically won the highest-profile case of the year, and this woman showed no emotion. He was not going to take it anymore. He followed Wendy to her office. He barged in and closed the door.

"Is everything OK with you?"

"Sure," she responded from her desk. "How can I help you?"

"You can help me by explaining your behavior," Noah vociferated. "You change from warm and fuzzy to ice cold in a matter of seconds. I can't read you!" Noah was hyperventilating with frustration.

Wendy waited for a few seconds before she responded. "Noah," she said, condescendingly. "Let's go over this one more time. You and I agreed last year our communication would be strictly professional. At the time we were not even under public scrutiny as we are now. Other than having a few drinks one night after work, nothing else has changed. If anything, the risk of people gossiping about you and me may be even greater. Are we on the same page?" Wendy wanted to emphasize her point. She never raised her voice or let her smile completely fade.

Noah did not answer.

"Please close the door after you leave," Wendy said, while looking at some papers on her desk.

Noah left and slammed the door.

A few hours later the court was ready to deliver the verdict.

Before leaving the office, Ms. Watson called an extraordinary meeting. Her speech was short, to the point, and with clear direction. "We are heading to the courtroom now. Despite winning or losing, I want absolutely no demonstration of emotion. Should we lose, the press could end our plaintiff business, severely affecting the firm. Should we win, a person is going to jail, and families will be affected; there is no reason for public demonstrations of joy. Are we clear?"

After a few seconds of silence, they headed to the courtroom.

Noah was still puzzled. Did Ms. Watson ever blink?

There were no surprises in the courtroom. Watson & Corcoran won the case. The media was all over the case and were hungry for comments and declarations.

The partners were all at the courthouse. They followed the precise instructions of Ms. Watson and headed to the office for a private but very deserved celebration.

Inside closed doors, the partners opened a bottle of champagne and celebrated with all the staff. Wendy and Noah received special mentions for their extensive hard work, long hours, and success.

The four partners stood at the head of the main conference room to offer a toast. Wendy and Noah were standing at the side, close to the table. Wendy had a discreet smile. She was happy for the firm, but she was only second chair in this trial. Noah instead had a wide smile and was shaking hands with everybody.

Mr. Koslow delivered a short speech about the highlights of the case and what winning meant for the firm. He raised his glass in honor of Wendy and Noah.

Mr. Adler silently raised his glass in sign of approval.

Mr. Corcoran was really excited. He hinted there was good news in the air for Noah. "We have many reasons to celebrate at Watson & Corcoran, so if everyone agrees, we should have an extracurricular company party this weekend. We may have some good news to share with you. I am sure the ice has already melted pretty much everywhere, so please tell me if you can make it to a celebration at Lake Minnetonka."

"Sounds like a great idea," said Mr. Koslow, seconding Mr. Corcoran's motion. We can take a ride on my sailboat."

"Better yet," Wendy interrupted, "Why don't we go to Bayfield? I am sure we can have a great time on Noah's boat. I've seen the pictures, and it's beautiful."

Noah felt like a bucket of cold ice had been dumped on his back.

"That sounds like a great idea," Noah responded. "Maybe we can do it at a different time. Bayfield is quite a drive from here..."

Wendy interrupted once again. "Driving? Who said anything about driving? Mr. Corcoran and you are pilots. Wouldn't it be fun if we could fly to Bayfield?"

Noah was looking at Wendy in disbelief. Why was she stabbing him this way?

"Wendy, that sounds like a great idea," Mr. Corcoran responded.

Noah had a fake smile in his face. He was sweating like never before.

Wendy was merciless. "Noah's got a place up there, so if he brings his wife some of us can stay at their place and some of us can stay in the hotels and make a great weekend out of it."

"Well, on such short notice, I am not sure we can find accommodations for all." Noah was fighting for his life.

"Oh, please," interrupted Wendy once again. "You are practically a hero there. I'm sure they'll find us fine lodging. C'mon, don't be so modest. Show us the great life you have there."

Ms. Watson was excited with the idea now. She really wanted to find a good cause that the firm could associate with. She had been following Noah's website and was excited about the good pro bono work he was doing and how many people had been benefiting from it. She would love to add to his effort and be able to help people in need, without involving a middleman.

She raised her hand indicating she wanted to talk.

Everybody quieted down.

"I am not sure Noah wants all of us there, and I wouldn't want to impose. However, if he does, Watson & Corcoran would be happy to attend. We would gladly reimburse him for the cost of the party and accommodations and even fuel for the plane if someone dares to fly with him or Mr. Corcoran. This was a critical case, and both Wendy and Noah worked really hard on it. I am happy to sponsor a big and very well-deserved celebration."

People started cheering and clapping. When they had quieted down, Wendy attacked once again: "Well, I'm flying with Mr. Blakely. Who else is joining us?"

"Ms. Thil," Ms. Watson interrupted. "I am sorry to interrupt you, but Mr. Blakely has not yet accepted to take this one on. Mr. Blakely?" Ms. Watson finished, looking at Noah. She still had not blinked even once since she had started speaking five minutes earlier.

"Mr. Blakely?" Ms. Watson insisted on the question.

"C'mon, c'mon, c'mon," Wendy was cheerfully whispering slyly.

"Sure, I'd be happy to," Noah responded, knowing from now on he was a dead man and that Wendy had killed him.

The crowd burst out with cheers and applauses.

Who Are You?

The cheers were still going.

"Wendy? Can we have a word in private?" Noah asked.

"Sure, let's go to my office," Wendy responded cheerfully. "The man can't stop working," she said to the crowd, to explain why she was taking him away from them into her office.

The glass door closed behind them.

"What are you doing?" Noah yelled at Wendy

"Shhhh," she warned him. Keep your voice down.

"You killed me. You know that?" he whispered, visibly upset and worried.

"Yes, and I enjoyed it," she said, with the same sarcastic smile she always had.

"Why?"

"Well, my dear Noah," she began calmly as she opened one of the drawers in her desk. "I have been busting my butt to get a promotion here for years. Suddenly they hired these two big-shot lawyers, newbies to the firm, and the rumor was that the only promotion coming up was going to be for one of them. So where does that leave me? Am I here just collecting dust? Is the implication that because I am a single mother, I can't have career aspirations?"

"Both are really good, one of them related to a partner of the firm. If I helped him, he would certainly be the winner, and I would be stuck at my job once again. However, if I helped the other one, only good things could happen. Either he would help me out after winning the promotion, or better yet, he could become an easy target so I could get him out of the way before getting the promotion myself. I would be the only experienced one left."

"You got me to believe you were really getting the promotion until you confessed all the lies you had been telling to get your way. You became an easy target."

"This is for you, my friend." She handed him an envelope.

"What's in it?"

"Insurance," she responded with a dry tone. "The day after we had our martinis—" Wendy interrupted herself: "Thanks for buying, by the way, I had a great time." She was her old sarcastic self again. "Anyway," she continued, "I came to the office and ran a query on the pages you looked at on your office computer."

"I didn't find a whole lot at the beginning, boat estimates, pilot lessons, estimates, and so on. Nothing really special, only that the dates are right after you talked to the different partners about your hobbies. That wasn't enough, but you made it really easy when you logged into the web developers' site—a couple of college kids. Really? All that master plan and preparation work and you didn't even hire a well-established business? Frankly, I'm a bit disappointed in you." Wendy's voice was soft, almost seductive, and her sentences ended with her typical slight smile. She was pulverizing Noah's world, and yet her facial expression was still sweet and tender."

Wendy kept on handing documents to Noah one at a time as supporting material to the points she was making.

"Nice college kids you hired, but they were somewhat concerned when I confronted them with impersonation of a city official from a different state. After all, they built a fake page for Bayfield, Wisconsin. They were especially concerned—they had a look almost as bad as the one you have in your eyes right now—when I told them that since their actions had gone across state borders this could easily escalate to a federal case. So they were happy to present this signed confession with the details of the operation: names, places, bills, instructions, etcetera. I told them I would represent them free of charge in case something went wrong, but that they shouldn't talk to you if they didn't want things to go even worse for them."

"Here is a copy of their declaration." Wendy kept on delivering documents as if they were a deck of cards.

Noah felt like crying. He felt deceived, worst of all deceived by a friend. His pulse was going faster by the minute.

"What do you want?" he asked, acknowledging defeat.

"Today is Tuesday. In theory you are piloting a plane on Friday to Bayfield to show us your boat and how people regard you as a hero there. You have until Thursday to resign and recommend me as the most suitable candidate for the promotion. Otherwise, you'll have to face your demons on Friday, and even if your enormous creativity pulls you out of this one, I have enough evidence to have you debarred."

"You were my friend. You were helping me!" Noah said in a defeated voice, trying to keep a straight face instead of crying helplessly.

"Are you of all people complaining because someone lied to you?" Wendy smiled sarcastically. "Noah, I was helping myself," interrupted Wendy in a soft, almost inaudible voice.

Noah remained silent. He felt his world collapsing. He felt betrayed. He felt like an idiot. He felt his blood pressure rising even higher.

"You don't have to respond now," Wendy said with her same sweet smile. "Why don't you go home to your wife and talk it over with her?"

"Grace!" he thought. How would he explain all this to her?

Noah felt shivers going down his spine. He was feeling dizzy and nauseous. He walked out of Wendy's office straight to his car and started driving home.

He couldn't focus. Should he concentrate on defending his reputation at the office? Or should he try to make a credible story for Grace? Maybe he needed to look for another job. But how could he explain that to Grace?

His mind tormented him with the consequences to come as he tried to find a way out of the mess he had created. On his drive home, he had to slam on the brakes since he failed to notice the car in front of him stopping at a red light. As he waited for the stoplight to turn green, he watched people walking across the street and imagined them pointing at him. "Liar!" they yelled, while pointing their index fingers right at his eyes. He heard Wendy laughing and enjoying his misery.

The car behind him honked and snapped him out of his thoughts. He arrived home trembling and sweating. He parked his car on the driveway and stumbled across the front yard.

Madelyn was playing outside with her toys.

"Madelyn!" he thought. How was he going to explain this to her? What if the media got a hold of this information? Would Madelyn grow up thinking her father was a liar? After all, the last case had been a high-profile one, and there were many in the media who might think this would be hot story.

His heart was beating faster than ever. He was short on breath and felt excruciating pressure in his chest.

Then all went black and silent.

Where Is the Tunnel?

Noah could see his body lying on the front yard of his house. Madelyn ran inside to call Grace.

"Somebody call an ambulance!" someone yelled. "Why is it that someone always says that instead of just calling one?" Noah thought.

One of the neighbors was pounding his chest animatedly, ordering him to breathe.

"It's funny," Noah thought, "nothing really hurts." He was enjoying this weightless, timeless, painless state.

Grace left the house and embraced his body, crying. He wanted to tell her he was fine and that there was no pain, but he couldn't. He couldn't move his body. Madelyn was crying too, and it hurt to see them suffering. However, the inability to tell them everything was OK was even more hurtful.

He could hear the ambulance approaching from a distance. He desperately tried to get into his body and let Grace know everything was OK, but it seemed to be blocked. He just couldn't get in.

Soon the ambulance came and they picked up his body and took it to the nearest hospital. He could only follow his body. This was really confusing. So, was he dead? Was this it?

Maybe if he were really dead, then he wouldn't have to deal with the mess he was in, but he wouldn't be able to be with Grace or Madelyn.

He saw his body lying in the hospital bed. Grace and Madelyn were crying in a room close to it while the doctors were plugging hoses and wires into his body. They were even cutting a hole in his chest. That looked like it should hurt, but it didn't.

So finally the light appeared. Was he supposed to walk toward it? What if it was the wrong light? This was the kind of situation where a wrong turn could really mess up things for quite a long time...

A voice came from where the light was. It was kind and gentle yet impossible to determine if it was a man or a woman's voice.

"It seems like you are in a big mess," said the voice.

"It surely does," Noah responded, looking at his opened body.

"Oh, yeah, that too, but the life you are leaving is a complete mess," responded the voice.

Noah remained silent for a while.

"Leaving?" he asked.

"Yes, it's time. Let's go," the voice indicated.

"No. Wait! What? Am I dead?" Noah asked.

"We don't exactly call it that."

"Regardless of what you call it, will I be able to see Grace and Madelyn again?"

"Not for a while."

"Please don't die, Daddy. Please don't die, Daddy. Please, please, please!" The voice of Madelyn interrupted Noah's chat with this voice.

"I don't want to go!" Noah yelled. "Is it my time?" he asked.

"Not really," the voice responded. "But the choices you had made in your life were leading you to a path that was not yours. So it's best if you leave now."

"Wait! What if I can make it better and return to my path, whatever that was?" Noah begged.

"OK. Let me think about that," the voice said, and vanished.

Noah looked at his body. Apparently he had been talking for hours. His body was already closed and peacefully resting by a few machines. He paid close attention to what the doctor was telling Grace.

"We did everything possible. He had a severe heart attack. His heart is not responding. So we have him connected to a respirator and will keep him alive for as long as possible, Ms. Blakely. But at this moment he is clinically dead."

Grace's sadness was breaking down Noah's spirit. The doctor left the room. Madelyn entered crying. "Is he going to be OK, Mom?"

"We hope so, sweetie."

And there was his body lying peacefully, with Madelyn and Grace standing nearby. There, in that room without anything else, he had everything he wanted; now he was about to lose it.

Someone knocked at the door and broke the peaceful moment.

"Ms. Blakely?"

"Yes?"

"My name is Wendy. I work with your husband. I am so sorry about what happened."

Grace looked at her. She paused for a while, and it was as though the two women were having a separate conversation with their eyes.

"Thanks," Grace said.

"Ms. Blakely, I am Mr. Corcoran. Your husband is a great man; he'll be able to overcome this turbulence." We have seen how good a captain he is, earning precious stripes as he succeeds professionally. I am sure this is just a temporary impasse and shortly we'll see him flying again.

"Thanks so much."

"Ms. Blakely, I am Mr. Koslow. I always admired the courage in your husband. These are troubled waters, but I am sure he'll navigate them successfully. He is a brave mariner. We are all very proud of him and sure he will be sailing back with us in no time."

"Thanks, you are so kind."

"Ms. Blakely, I am Ms. Watson. You husband has given so much to people in need. I am sure many people will be praying for a quick recovery."

"I really appreciate all of you taking time to come and see him," Grace replied.

In the meantime, Wendy was discreetly checking out the respirator, the catheters, and Noah's pulse.

Noah couldn't believe it. She was actually thinking he made this up as an escape from Friday's deadline. Actually, Noah thought, it would have been almost a viable solution...

Grace was not comfortable with the proximity of Wendy to Noah's body.

"The doctor says he is in a coma, and we still don't know what's going to happen," Grace said while looking at Wendy.

Wendy got the message and stepped away. "I am sure he will recover shortly."

"Please don't die, Daddy. Please don't die, Daddy. Please, please, please!" Somehow, Madelyn's voice overpowered every other audible voice. In fact, she was quietly praying, but it was all Noah could hear.

The light brightened up the area again.

"Since it's still not your time, you'll have a chance to redo some of your steps. Here are the rules. The moment you fail to follow them, that will be the end of your second chance.

"You have to make your lies, the truth. You made up some stories. Now you have to make them real.

"You can tell no one about this, no matter how hard it is.

"Your time is limited to when your loved ones decide it's over.

"This is not going to be easy. All I can tell you is that only by dropping what's not important can you keep what really matters."

Before Noah could accept, decline, or ask for any further explanation, the voice was gone again; but nothing else happened, at least for a short while.

The First Truth

The next thing he knew, he was sitting in his office, in absolute silence. Noah was looking around trying to figure out what was going on. He knew where he was; he didn't know *when* it was.

"Have you decided on a boat?" Mr. Koslow interrupted the silence in Noah's office. "Don't wait for the summer to end."

Mr. Koslow's voice startled him. He remembered Koslow had said that, but he was lost for a few seconds. Why was Mr. Koslow asking for it again?

Noah lifted his eyes to the wall where he had placed the fake pictures of the boat, but the wall was empty.

"How are you enjoying yours?" Noah responded almost reflexively. He did not elaborate on the answer, at least not this time.

Mr. Koslow kept going on about boating. Noah kept engaged in the conversation. He remembered that was one of his main goals, and he had to keep up with it. At the moment, what he really wanted was to go home and hug Grace and Madelyn.

Noah took off early that afternoon. He arrived home and embraced Grace strongly for a while. Some tears even dropped down his cheek. He discreetly wiped them off.

Grace was surprised. An over-effusive hug? Coming home early from work?

"Is everything OK?" Grace asked.

"Yes, sure. Just missed you. It's been so long..."

"What do you mean so long?" Grace asked. They had had sex that morning. She probably had to do better next time so he wouldn't have forgotten about it by midafternoon, she thought to herself.

Noah did not continue the conversation. Last he knew he was about to die and couldn't hug her. He knew he had a limited time to fix the mess he was in.

"We should go to the cabin for the Fourth. Would you like that?" he asked, changing the topic.

"Oh, that would be wonderful," Grace agreed.

While she went grocery shopping for the up-coming weekend, Noah jumped on the phone with the boat dealer. He didn't know how much time he had to fix this mess, to make those lies become truths, but he knew it was limited.

"How much did you say it costs?" he screamed.

"Three hundred thousand," said the Crownline dealer. "This beauty comes with a bedroom, a fully equipped kitchen and living room, the engine is a…"

"Sorry to interrupt you, Scott," Noah said.

"Scooter," the dealer said, correcting Noah.

"Whatever. What financing do you have on this thing?"

"We've got a special right now. 20 percent down and 5.99 percent interest for up to seventy-two months, on approved credit." He sounded like a TV ad.

"That would amount to sixty thousand dollars down and seventy-two easy payments of around four thousand dollars plus tax. Isn't that a sweet deal? We can even deliver it to any place state-wide at no charge."

"Can you put it in Bayfield's marina for this weekend?"

"Sure, I just need you to stop by, sign the papers, and take care of some documents, Mr. Blakely."

"I'll be there tomorrow morning," Noah said. His voice did not have the excitement of a guy who just bought his first boat.

As planned, they went to the cabin during the long weekend. Noah also surprised his family with a boat ride, as he had done last year. He failed to mention that he had actually purchased it.

He would come clean...after the long drive home. The car was a confined space, and he wouldn't want to have that as a location for a lecture from Grace.

It was certainly much more that he could afford. But it was absolutely beautiful. He knew that even if there ever was a possibility that he could be in a position to own a boat, by diving into this kind of debt now he would never be able to really afford one.

However, the best thing he could do now was to enjoy the time with his family, to memorize every laugh of Madelyn and her sense of wonder, to tell her stories about mermaids in Lake Superior, to enjoy a quiet evening with Grace.

"Captain Noah" was cruising well off into Lake Superior. Madelyn and Grace were wondering about the beautiful thirty-six-foot yacht, but they were also shooting pictures of everything they saw and having the time of their lives.

At lunchtime they sat on the deck. As Grace was serving lunch, Noah fainted. Grace helped him to lie down. Noah was breathing normally.
Grace was starting to panic.

For a few seconds, Noah was watching the scene. He was peacefully resting while Grace was trying to wake him up.

A blink of an eye later, he was watching his body at the hospital. It took him a while to understand that he was again seeing himself before returning to his life to make his lies truths.

Grace was talking with the doctor.

"There is nothing else we can do, Ms. Blakely. He is in a coma; he is alive because he is connected to all these instruments. It's up to you if we keep him like that or let him go. Please bear in mind that keeping him like this comes not only at a very high financial cost but also an emotional one."

Grace was crying inconsolably when Wendy and Ms. Watson entered the room to pay him a visit.

"Hello, Ms. Blakely," Ms. Watson said. "We are colleagues of Mr. Blakely."

Grace kept on crying. "I am going to have to let him die," she said. "I cannot afford to keep him like this much longer..." And she left the room as if she wanted to run away from the whole situation as well.

"Can we help her out?" Wendy asked Ms. Watson.

"What do you mean?"

"Well, he is still technically an employee of the firm. Can we help out with his hospital bills?"

"That is very nice of you, but he is technically on medical leave. We are obliged to pay a portion of his salary for a couple of months but not for his medical bills." Ms. Watson explained accurately the firm's policies to Wendy.

"I understand," Wendy said. "But is it possible to make an exception and help him out, as a charitable donation for example?"

"Charity is better when aimed at those who are alive," said Ms. Watson. "Just to clear the firm of any liabilities, we will pay his medical leave salary and two months of hospital bills, but that's it."

"That bitch," Noah thought. And Wendy, did she feel so guilty she was interceding on his behalf?

Two months, that's all he had before somebody would literally pull the plug on him. Noah knew Grace was running low on money and would have to choose to protect Madelyn's future over hospital bills to keep him alive in an indefinite coma. Ms. Watson had authorized Wendy for two months of hospital bills. Two to three months was all he had to make his lies truths!

In the blink of an eye, he was back on Lake Superior, waking up from a short faint.

"What happened to you?" Grace yelled.

"Why?"

"You fainted."

"Really?"

"Nothing really happened."

"Are you OK? Are you sick?"

"I'm just fine. Let's eat!"

"Will you visit the doctor next week?"

"Sure, I'll see the doctor shortly if that makes you happy."

After the long weekend was over they returned home. They had an amazing time. Noah wasn't sure he was going to be able to turn his lies into truths, so at the very least he wanted to enjoy every second with his family.

Noah didn't want to risk lying about the boat to Grace. He knew he had to tell her he had bought it, so he tried to make the delivery of the message less painful—for both of them.

"You know," he said, when there was about an hour left of the drive back. "Wouldn't it be great to open a bottle of the Golden Gris wine you like so much and relax for a while in the hot tub?"

"Hmmm, yeah, it sounds great," Grace said, while grabbing Noah's hand.

Madelyn had fallen fast asleep in the car. When they arrived home it was easy to take her to her bedroom and let her continue sleeping. She was really tired from a long and very active weekend.

Grace prepared the bath and brought in a bottle of Golden Gris. Noah came in a few minutes later with some candles—and a couple of more bottles.

"Honey, you have to work tomorrow," Grace said.

Noah didn't respond. He just opened the first bottle and joined Grace in the tub.

They chatted about everything. Their life together, their plans for the future, Madelyn, a potential sibling for Madelyn...

Grace had hardly any body fat, and two glasses of wine would get her buzzed. Noah was well aware of that, and he sweet-talked her into having almost three times that much.

"Honey, remember the boat we used this weekend?"

"Shh-uu-re," Grace responded with an aimless look and a lost smile.

"Did you like it?"

"Shh-uu-re..."

"Well, what do you know. I bought it!" Noah said while laughing loudly.

Grace laughed with him.

"Rrreally?" Grace asked after a while.

"Really what?"

"Did you buy it?"

"Yeees!" Noah responded, laughing again.

Grace joined him in his laughter.

Noah left early for work the next morning, before anybody had woken up.

His tactic was a good way to delay the inevitable with some added "benefit." When he arrived home, Grace still had a bad hangover, which had her in a crabby mood.

"Did you say yesterday that you had actually purchased the boat?"

"Sure, honey," Noah responded as if it was no big deal. "Where is Madelyn?" And he headed toward the backyard.

"What?"

"Where is Madelyn?" he repeated.

"Funny," Grace said, with an expression that was completely different from the word. "Did you buy the boat?"

"Yes."

"Are you completely out of your mind?"

"I am crazy about you; does that count?"

"I don't even know how much you paid for it... but return it. We don't need it. We have other expenses, real important ones. What about the mortgage? What about Madelyn's college?"

"Is she already in college? Well, there you go. Four more years and she'll be able to help us with the mortgage." Noah thought cracking a quick joke could ease the pain.

Grace went at it for a while, and Noah was not confrontational at all. When allowed, he spoke and tried to position the boat purchase as a way to enjoy family fun and build great memories with Madelyn. He tried to ease Grace's worries by telling her things were going well at work and that they were young and healthy.

Noah's only way out was to compromise. He said if things were not going well by next year, he would sell the boat and forget about it. In the back of his mind, he knew he only had two to three months. After that, the real him would be disconnected and all this life he was dealing with would disappear. At least that's what he understood of what that voice had told him the day of his heart attack.

After the agreement, they looked at the pictures and had yet another wonderful evening.

The Second Truth

So the financial future was grim. Between the boat payments, the car payments, the mortgage, and all the other expenses, it was easy to see a collapse in the near future. Noah, however, was very focused. He needed to take care of three things in two months: the luxury boat, (checked), the pilot's license, (work in progress), and the "hero" status in Bayfield (not even started).

The next morning Noah already had a few estimates off of the Internet on the private pilot's license process. He signed up for the "Accelerated Flight Training" class. Provided there was good weather and he could quickly learn the ground training, he could have a license in less than two months.

This would set him back about fifteen thousand dollars he didn't have and most of the time he had left. Well, the banks were always willing to lend some money, at a cost, of course; and it seemed easier to tackle this one first. The "hero" status, well, that seemed more complicated.

Work at the office was really busy, and Noah could not allow Joshua to shine more than him.

He had pretty much discounted any conversation with Wendy.

Noah's office was decorated with real pictures now, and his extracurricular conversations with Mr. Koslow and Mr. Corcoran were even more interesting now that he really knew what he was talking about.

After a few days Noah completed the ground training. The workload was almost unbearable, especially taking into account not only the hours studying and his long workdays, but the competition against Joshua and the stress of a deadline (literally speaking). Grace started complaining about Noah's absence from home. Noah knew things would get worse as he advanced toward the pilot lesson. He needed to complete at the very least thirty flight hours.

Inevitably, Grace started questioning his absence.

"I am taking a class," Noah said, trying to justify it.

"What kind of a class? Is it for work?"

"It's intended to build a common ground between one of the partners and me."

"Oh, so is it a mentoring session of some sort?"

"You could call it that."

"How long will this take?"

"A couple of months. Why am I under this line of questioning?"

"Because I barely see you anymore. Because Madelyn and I need time with you. Because I am not the only parent that Madelyn has. How many more reasons do you need? Is this a satisfactory answer to your concern about my 'line of questioning'?" Grace made air quotes and used a tone that clearly explained her frustration.

There was silence for a while. Noah did not want to get into any arguments with Grace. He understood perfectly how she must feel, but he also knew he couldn't provide her with just any explanation, based on the marching orders he had.

Grace wasn't one who just left a conversation like this up in the air.

"I am sorry," she apologized. "I know you are under a lot of stress," Grace said, as she came close to Noah and hugged him remorsefully. "So what's this class about?" .

Noah was too afraid to lie. Even disguising the truth was treading a very fine line. However, he knew she would not stop with the first explanation he'd given, and the voice had been very clear about not mentioning this second chance to anybody.

"I can't tell you."

Things inevitably got much worse. The training included night flights, so Noah had to be out late at night. He blamed it on the class but still provided no additional explanation.

More and more cases came across his desk. For some reason, these cases were different from the ones he had done before, so his previous research was useless. The combination of the time devoted to the cases plus the unpredictable weather patterns did not help to speed up the process of getting his pilot's license. Noah needed to have time available in his schedule to fly, and he had to make it coincide with his instructor's availability, and all of this had to happen on days with good weather.

He was absent from his house on weekends and most weekday evenings. Grace was irritable and constantly upset. On the few nights Noah was home, he looked tired and absent. Sex and the surprises she liked so much were things of the past. She started suspecting Noah was having an affair. The mere thought of it made her stomach turn.

She thought about following him to catch him red-handed, but what would the purpose be? Was there really something going on, or was it just a product of her imagination?

The day was approaching. That Saturday, Noah was about to complete his last flight hour required to obtain his license. Sadly, he had no one to celebrate with. At least he was going home and enjoying a nice lunch with his family. He was well aware of the tense atmosphere around Grace. All told, it had been fast, just under three months.

Lunches were nothing like a while ago. They were silent, other than the clanking of the silverware hitting the dishes and an occasional pouring of juice or water. The joy of the family was coming apart fast.

As Noah was heading to the table, he fainted again. Grace was in the kitchen, so she did not notice. Madelyn was in her room, unaware that her dad was home. She was used to it by now.

Noah looked at his body lying on the carpet by the couch for a few seconds, and then he saw his body in the hospital again. He had almost forgotten about this scenery by now.

Grace was by his side. She had lost a lot of weight and had deep black circles under her eyes. The doctor came into the room.

"It's time," she said. "The firm suspended payments last month, and I simply can't afford to keep this going on." She cried inconsolably.

"Would you prefer to wait outside?" the doctor asked.

"No, I want to be here until he goes..."

Noah started to feel out of breath as the doctor made the final approach to disconnect him from the respirator.

Someone knocked at the door. It was Wendy.

"Doctor," she said. "Please don't do it. I was able to negotiate with the firm to keep on paying for his treatment for a while."

The doctor looked at Grace.

"Thank you!" Grace said, as she embraced Wendy, still crying.

Noah thought this was very strange. Why would Ms. Watson change her mind? She never did before.

Wendy's phone vibrated.

"Yes," she said, "please continue to send the billing to the same address. Just change the addressee from Watson & Corcoran to Ms. Wendy Thil and label it 'Personal and Confidential.' Thanks."

"Wow," thought Noah. Wendy was paying for it now. That was a shocker. He had a bit more appreciation for her, but after all, she was the one who pushed him down this abyss.

Noah woke up from his faint in the living room. This time nobody had noticed. It was kind of sad.

Despite all the attempts to alleviate the tension, despite Noah exercising his best charm and wit, lunch was as boring as they all had become. He wished he could explain everything to Grace, he wished he could tell her how important Madelyn and she were in his life, and he wished he could tell her that regardless of the appearances, he was doing this with them in mind.

Another day, another battle; at least he had conquered the second truth. Now he needed to focus on the third one. There was no doubt this was the hardest one. Why did he allow himself to get into this mess?

Third Time Is a Charm

Learning something is easy, buying something is even easier, but becoming a person respected by a community requires serious work. This endeavor was going to take all he had, all he had learned, and all he could invent.

Noah started going to Bayfield over the weekends. At least the pilot lessons allowed him to fly over there instead of driving. He needed to do some research, but of course these weekend trips didn't help his relationship with Grace at all.

Flying over the turning fall colors was one of those small rewards he could enjoy in this puzzled life he was living. The noise of the engine humming faded in his head as he dreamed of how nice things were for him. He tried not to think about the uncertain deadline he had. It all depended on Wendy continuing to pay for the costs of the hospital keeping him alive in his other life; what an irony!

Noah spent the weekend in Bayfield. This time, unlike weekends he'd spent there in the past, he actually devoted his time to looking at the town, its people and their needs. It was a small town by comparison to Minneapolis. He spent the weekend observing, talking with residents, and taking notes. Sunday afternoon he flew back to Minneapolis after reading his notes and going over the pictures. He wanted to make a positive change in Bayfield, but beyond his need to overcome a previous lie, he also wanted to genuinely help out the community.

Sunday night he arrived home to a very upset Grace. They hardly spoke a word. He noticed a couple of empty bottles in the recycling bin.

"Sorry I missed the celebration," he said, trying to joke with Grace. Grace did not respond.

Noah understood things were not going well with Grace. He tried unsuccessfully to approach her and start patching things up. The plan backfired when Grace, with pent-up anger, broke the silence and started an interrogation.

"So you think you could just take off for a whole weekend and things would be just peachy when you returned? You have been absent from our lives for a long time, and all I get when I ask for an explanation are vague answers. You have responsibilities as a husband and as a father that you are not fulfilling. I don't care how important your job is. Nothing should be more important than keeping your family together."

"Grace, I know it's hard for you to believe me, but the purpose of everything that I am doing right now is precisely to keep us together." Noah's tone was calm and reassuring, as opposed to Grace's bellicose one.

"Can you tell me what is it that you are doing?"

"No, I can't."

"See? That's what I am talking about. You pushed me out of your life, and you can't tell me why."

"It will be over soon."

"When?"

"I don't know exactly."

"Well, I'm not good at ultimatums, Noah, but take this as one. If you really want Madelyn and me in your life, you have to let us in your life. I don't think what we are living through is fair, nor do we deserve it."

With that, Grace added yet more pressure to Noah's situation.

He didn't sleep that night. He was getting used to sleepless nights. At least by the next morning he had a draft of his idea to fix his third lie. The idea of getting over with this was so intoxicatingly good that for the moment, Noah left Grace's ultimatum unattended.

The following day Noah started to execute his next plan. During his commute to work in the morning, he called the Wisconsin Public Radio station asking for an appointment to pitch his idea. A few days later he was on the phone with the advertising manager of the station stating the generalities of the idea. Noah also offered to fly into Madison, WPR's headquarters, that Friday so they could meet in person and finalize the details.

The first part of his plan consisted of giving away his boat. He would still owe the debt to the bank, but he would raffle the boat, selling two thousand tickets at $250 each. The raffle would only take place when the two thousandth ticket was sold.

After paying for the advertising fees to WPR, the remainder of the money would go to purchasing and remodeling a building in Bayfield. The building would then become a licensed daycare center for children of single moms. They would be able to leave their kids at this center free of charge while going to work.

WPR loved the idea and jumped right on it.

"Do you have a name for the project?"

"The Grace Center," Noah responded.

He flew directly from Madison to Bayfield that night so he could get an early start on Saturday. The city hall was open. They provided guidance on vacant lots and rundown buildings that might be available. Noah designed some fliers to create awareness of the upcoming raffle and dropped them around town in coffee shops, libraries, and schools.

Sunday morning he headed back to Minneapolis. He wanted to spend some time with Grace. It was evident things were not going well, and spending yet another weekend away right after their "talk" wasn't the best move. At least if he could be home for most of Sunday things might improve a bit.

Noah was due home right before noon. He stopped by Broder's Restaurant, Grace's favorite. He ordered two lobster lasagnas to go. He had bought two bottles of Golden Gris in Wisconsin, since local rules did not allow alcohol sales in Minnesota on Sundays. Ironically, Golden Gris was a wine made in Hastings, Minnesota, and Noah had to buy it in Wisconsin.

Noah returned to an empty home.

He saw a knocked-off bottle of Golden Gris on the dining table with an empty wineglass standing by it.

The picture frame that used to hold his wedding picture was standing by the glass of wine, but instead of the usual picture it had a white paper with one word written across it: "Goodbye."

He grabbed his cell phone and called Grace. His fingers were trembling with desperation, and the tears in his eyes were making the image on the screen blurry. He heard Grace's phone ringing. It was by her night table—with another note—"Don't look for us."

Right next to the phone there was another empty wineglass. The leftover drops fell like tears over its inner walls, piling up around the circumference of the wedding ring lying on the bottom.

There was a carefully wrapped box on his night table. It looked like a fancy shirt box, and it had a little card on top. The card read, "For you." It was in Grace's handwriting.

Noah tore the paper wrapping and found a nice Montblanc fountain pen. It was sitting on top of some papers with a sticky flag indicating,
"Sign Here:" It was the divorce papers.

Grace asked for nothing except for full custody of Madelyn.

Noah felt defeated and sad. All this effort, for nothing; he had lost what was his most precious treasure. He had lost the only two women he cared for in his life. He had no idea what to do. He could only imagine how much suffering had he inflicted on Grace.

He was ready to tell her the whole thing, even if that meant dying in his other life. What if this was his only life with her? Had he then wasted the previous months and irreparably damaged his relationship with her?

He spent a few hours trying to figure out where Grace could be; but he also knew Grace was a pretty smart woman. He would not be able to find her if she didn't want to be found.

He cried himself to sleep.

Lessons from the Past

Noah woke up the next day still dressed; he was hugging Grace's pillow, now swamped in tears. It was just a few weeks before Thanksgiving, just when every ad and every person reminds you how important family is.

He remembered it was exactly a year ago when he had taken Grace and Madelyn on a trip to Bayfield. He remembered the smile on Grace's face when she found the necklace.

The house felt really empty. There was an echo all around. Madelyn's laughter was no longer there. Noah even missing Grace's nagging.

At this point he was not even sure if he was dead or alive, and if he was alive, which one was his real life? Was it the one where he was lying in bed connected to countless tubes and machines to keep him breathing? Or was it the one where he was hugging a pillow, had just lost his wife and kid, and was heading toward bankruptcy?

He went to work that morning, not because he wanted to, but because he knew of nothing else he could do.

The fast pace at the office helped him take his mind away from his miserable reality and focus on doing his job and on building strong bonds with the senior partners.

At lunchtime he was supposed to meet with Joshua and Wendy about a case they were working on. As he was heading to their table, Mr. Koslow interrupted his path.

"Have you prepared your boat for winter yet? It's a very common mistake for novices to forget that."

"I'm doing it this weekend," Noah responded.

"It's always sad knowing you have to wait for a few months before the next boat trip," Koslow continued, obviously in the mood for some boat talk.

"I know what you mean, Mr. Koslow, but I decided to give away my boat."

"What? You just bought it."

"Yes, but I found an opportunity to make something better out of it. So I decided to organize a raffle and with the profits build a community center in Bayfield," Noah said, as he pulled out of his pocket a couple of tickets.

"Are you serious? C'mon, have a seat." Mr. Koslow was stunned.

Mr. Koslow sat at the table where Ms. Watson was seating.

"You've got to hear this," Mr. Koslow told Ms. Watson, while pointing at Noah.

This was a golden opportunity for Noah's goal, and he was not going to let it pass, especially now that it was true. Slowly, Noah started to explain the generalities of the program and how it would benefit a weak segment of the community. He next explained the specifics of the raffle and then continued to relate the next steps.

"This weekend, I'm going back to Bayfield to kick off a parallel initiative called PAC. That's short for 'Park-Away Campaign.' It's aimed at making people conscious about leaving parking spots close to the doors of the stores empty in case someone such as a single mother, someone in a real hurry, or anyone with a need higher than theirs requires it.

Noah had drafted that idea in his head on the flight back Sunday night, and somehow while sitting at the table with Mr. Koslow and Ms. Watson, it just came out as if he had been planning it for a while.

Ms. Watson loved Noah's initiatives and suggested that he place copies of the raffle tickets on the company bulletin board. That was a highly visible place, and up to now no one had dared to place anything on that board that wasn't related to work. Ms. Watson also bought a few tickets and promised him her support in promoting them. She even cracked a smile.

Mr. Koslow was impressed and of course followed Ms. Watson's lead.

"Put me down for a couple of tickets," he said. "Who knows? Maybe I'll be able to own your boat."

Wendy and Joshua watched from a distance. Joshua was extremely uncomfortable with the proximity of Noah with the senior partners.

Discreetly, as if she wanted to catch up on her email, Wendy pulled out her phone. "Meeting postponed forty-five minutes," Wendy texted Noah. She did not want to interrupt his pitch to the senior partners.

Wendy had arrived early to the conference room.

"So how did it go?" She fired the question as soon as Noah entered the room.

"How did what go?" Understandably, Noah had all barriers up when addressing Wendy.

"Well, your 'chat' with Mr. Koslow and Ms. Watson. I even saw Ms. Watson smiling. Can I tell you a key piece of info about her?" Wendy asked in a whispering voice.

"Not really. It's best if we don't really talk behind the senior partner's back, don't you think so?" Noah cut her off abruptly.

There was an uncomfortable silence for a few minutes until Joshua arrived and broke it.

"I saw you were scoring some good points with the bigwigs," he said.

"You think so?" Noah dismissed the remark and began to disclose the topics on the meeting's agenda.

Toward the end of the day, as Noah was leaving the office, Wendy caught up with him in the hallway.

"Big plans for tonight?" she asked.

Noah was about to dismiss the question with a snappy comment when something caught their attention. There was a heated discussion over by the partners' offices. Wendy and Noah slowed down their pace discreetly to try to figure out what was going on.

They couldn't really understand the wording, but they could tell that it was Joshua's voice and that the counterpart was his uncle Mr. Adler.

"A little family argument?" Wendy asked with a bit of a smirk.

"Who knows?" Noah responded.

"Hey, are you upset with me?" Wendy protested.

"Not really, excuse me. It has been a long few weeks and the workload from the office, plus the fundraiser, is draining most of my energy. I am just tired." Noah snuck his way out of an argument with Wendy.

Even if she didn't fully buy it, the argument had some basis to it.

The next few weeks went by slowly. Noah cried almost every night and wrote love notes to an imaginary Grace, hoping one day she would read them.

Every weekend he went to Bayfield to work on his programs. People were starting to recognize him. Many were slowly starting to follow the PAC initiative. It was shaping the community. People who really needed a closer parking spot the most were able to get it because other ones were willing and able to walk a few more feet. This wasn't a law; there wasn't a sign posted in the parking lots.

It was a growing trend communicated by word of mouth. It appealed to the community members' willingness to do good because they wanted to, not because it was mandated.

The construction site for Grace Center had already been selected, and ticket sales were approaching two thousand faster than Noah estimated. Noah met often with the local authorities at city hall. While they were thrilled about this effort and Noah's generosity, they were also very curious about the motivation for it. Noah insisted all he wanted was to make a difference within the community, and he saw a chance to ask for a piece of the puzzle he needed.

Noah wondered if it would be OK to put up a website that would post the progress of the different initiatives. He wanted to gather comments from users about what they liked and how Noah's projects might be improved. However, Noah had learned his lesson from the past, so he ran the idea by the authorities.

The local authorities not only agreed to the website but offered to set it up free of charge. Noah provided them with the domain name www.bayfield.us, and the Bayfield officials took care of all the other expenses.

"Another milestone achieved," Noah thought. He was still unsure if it was worth it or not, but it was his only choice at the moment.

It was now the last week before Christmas vacation. While things at work were thriving, solitude was driving Noah into a deep depression. He had not heard a word from Grace or Madelyn and missed them every second.

Wendy stopped by his office the last day, just before leaving.

"Hey, we can take off now. How about dinner? My treat."

"Sure," Noah agreed. He really had nothing else to do.

They had a great time. The food was great, and the conversation was lively and witty. Noah always liked Wendy's sarcasm.

She ordered a couple of martinis.

"Sorry, can't drink," Noah declined.

"Why?"

"I am flying tomorrow to Bayfield. Can't drink before flying."

"Well, then, I'll drink both martinis," Wendy responded.

"So, tell me a bit about you, Mr. Mystery Man." Wendy started asking personal questions after her second martini.

"Not much to tell," he responded. "I am happily married to Grace and we have a daughter, Madelyn." His voice broke a little when he mentioned Madelyn's name.

Even though Wendy was buzzed she picked on it.

"Everything OK with Madelyn?"

"Sure!"

"What about you?"

"I have two beautiful kids, ages eight and ten. I used to be happily married, and for the past four years, I have been happily divorced."

"That's completely new information," Noah thought to himself.

The two martinis became four, and Wendy was pretty drunk by the end of the night. She revealed information about her divorce and a couple of other broken relationships, one of them with a colleague in her previous job. That was the reason why she had taken this job. Noah was making mental notes, just in case he would need that information later on. He had not forgotten whom he was dealing with and what was she capable of doing.

The restaurant closed, and it was evident that Wendy couldn't drive home. Noah became then the designated driver. He helped her into her house, and as he was preparing to leave, Wendy gave him a hug, thanking him for the ride. While hugging him she asked, "Is there a rule against passengers in your plane who've been drinking the night before?"

"What do you mean?"

"Can you take me to Bayfield tomorrow? If you want you can spend the night here."

"Thanks, Wendy, you are very kind, but I am happily married and intend to stay that way." With that he left before his will broke. After all, he really liked Wendy and technically he was already separated—at least in this life.

Wendy didn't let go of him, and he hesitated momentarily, but using his last ounce of will, he left.

Grateful Grace

Back in his other life, he was still lying in bed, immersed in a coma. Grace would come as often as possible to visit him, sometimes with Madelyn.

Right after the holidays Grace decided to pay a visit to Watson & Corcoran. She thought it was the least she could do. If it weren't for their generosity she would have had to disconnect Noah a long time ago.

She drove to downtown Minneapolis and walked into the fancy building where Noah used to work. The person in the front desk announced her to Ms. Watson.

Ms. Watson had Grace wait in the lobby for a few minutes. In the meantime she asked Wendy for Noah's medical file.

"Why do you need it?"

"His wife is here. I don't want any surprises. Let me review his file."

She glanced at it. Everything seemed to be in order.

"Please, let Ms. Blakely in," she asked the clerk in the lobby.

"Ms. Watson."

"Ms. Blakely."

"I am Noah's wife, and I just want to take a few minutes of your time," Grace said, while standing in the doorway of Ms. Watson's fancy office.

"Sure, Ms. Blakely, please come on in and have a seat." Ms. Watson pointed at the sofa at one side of her office. "May I offer you something to drink?"

"No, thank you, Ms. Watson. I know you are very busy, and I don't want to take much of your time. I am just coming to thank you for your generosity. Without it I would have to have had Noah disconnected a long time ago." Grace's voice broke as she finished her sentence.

Ms. Watson was silent for a few seconds. She looked confused. "I'll bring you a glass of water," she said, as she walked to her desk. She poured a glass of water and reached for Noah's file. As she walked the five steps back to the sofa, she opened the file and read the relevant portion.

"Ms. Blakely, I understand how nerve-wracking your situation must be. Noah's contributions to Watson & Corcoran were extremely valuable, and he was highly regarded by all of us. While I appreciate your gratitude to the firm regarding the hospital bills, we certainly do not deserve it. I just double-checked Noah's file. We followed standard procedure for this case, and while we extended his benefits by subsidizing the first two months of hospital bills, we suspended them after that."

"I don't understand. I'm confused," responded Grace.

"I understand Mr. Blakely had done significant charity work. Do you think it's possible someone from this charity has been paying for the bills?"

"Charity?" Grace asked, still more confused.

"Yes, for single mothers in the Bayfield area, I understand. Didn't you know about it?" Ms. Watson responded, intrigued.

Grace was deeply confused about Noah's parallel life, his role as mysterious benefactor and his reasons for taking on that role. Life had been really complicated for her, and just now it was starting to level off. She had lost her house and the nice cars, but now she was finding stability with Madelyn. The thought of having unpaid hospital bills accumulating for months was almost as devastating as having to deal with the decision about letting Noah go and giving up hope.

She excused herself and stormed out of Ms. Watson's office, heading straight to the hospital.

Grace demanded Noah's records, and she found out that even though the bills were sent to the same address, the payment came from Ms. Wendy Thil, not from Watson & Corcoran. Why was Wendy Thil paying for it? Had something actually happened between them?

She asked at accounting within the hospital about the payments. All they knew was that the payments came on time and that everything was covered until the end of January.

It was getting late in the day, and Grace did not want to continue the anguish of not knowing for another day. She ran back to the office. This time, she did not stop at the lobby or wait to be announced.

She just let herself in and started reading names on people's doors. She had never seen a picture of Wendy, and now she was more curious about her looks.

Finally she arrived at Wendy's door.

"Are you Ms. Wendy Thil?"

"Yes, can I help you?"

"I am Grace Blakely. Can you explain to me why are you paying for my husband's hospital bills?"

"Please have a seat."

Grace was not about to calm down. She felt a bit self-conscious; not only had she been running back and forth between the office and the hospital, but the last year had been really rough on her life. Wendy, on the other hand, looked great. Even late in the afternoon, her hair still looked wonderful, her skin looked fresh, and for sure she was wearing the latest fashion available.

"I am not having a seat. Were you having an affair with my husband?"

"Of course not!"

Their voices were loud, and there weren't too many people left in the building. Soon Ms. Watson and the other partners came to see what was going on.

Wendy took control of the situation, and although she was upset, she spoke courteously yet firmly.

"Ms. Blakely, I knew the firm was not going to pay for Noah's hospital bills. You had also indicated you were having some financial concerns, so I decided to help Noah. I did not want to make it public, nor do I want anything in return. I hope you can understand people are entitled to do good deeds without making them public. Now if you will please excuse me, I have work to do."

"Ms. Thil, I have lost every material possession I had. I lost my husband. Whether you had something going on with him or not, I'll never know, but at the very least, allow me to keep my dignity. If I cannot afford to pay for his bills, so be it. I do not need your charity," Grace said with tears in her eyes and a broken voice. She turned around, and the partners open a path for her, as if she were making an honorable exit.

After she left there was silence at Wendy's office. Nobody talked, but all were looking at Wendy.

"So was that how you used your raise after the promotion?" Koslow asked, to break the ice.

Wendy just looked at him.

"Ms. Thil, were you having an affair with Mr. Blakely?" Ms. Watson asked. "Before you respond, bear in mind that even with him no longer present at the office, that is not permissible behavior at Watson & Corcoran.

"If you can excuse me for a moment," Mr. Adler interrupted, "I will be right back."

"Ms. Watson," Wendy responded calmly, enunciating each and every word. "My relationship with Mr. Blakely was strictly professional and limited to the walls of this office. I find it troubling and offensive that you are even considering the words of an unstable and irritated woman."

"Excuse me, I am back," Mr. Adler interrupted. He had an envelope in his hand. "These may shed some light on the situation," he said as he pulled some pictures out of the envelope. He started rotating them through the partners. "These are from last year. I was at a restaurant and was severely disturbed by an intoxicated couple. They were drunk and disturbing other customers as well. Then I realized it was Mr. Blakely and Ms. Thil. My guess is that their relationship was not limited to the walls of this office. As you can see, Ms. Thil looks intoxicated. Oh, and this one is Mr. Blakely helping Ms. Thil into his car. They left together."

"Ms. Thil, is that you in the pictures?" Ms. Watson asked.

"I can explain."

"Please respond to my question." Ms. Watson cut short Wendy's intended explanation.

"Yes, that's me, but..."

Ms. Watson was ready to bring a high-profile case to the firm. Public displays of intoxicated team members and the potential rumor of an extramarital affair could really affect the firm's image in the following days. The press was going to be all over this. What if someone else had documented this? What if it was true they were in a relationship and had been seen in public somewhere else? This was not a risk she wanted to expose the firm to.

"Ms. Thil," Ms. Watson interrupted. She waited for everyone to be completely silent, and then looked at Wendy with a grave and serious expression. "Your behavior is questionable, and you were clearly intoxicated in public with a married member of the firm. That's not something we particularly applaud here at Watson & Corcoran. In addition, you just lied to all the partners by indicating your relationship with Mr. Blakely was limited to the walls of this office. Please be sure to clear your office by tomorrow before 5:00 p.m."

Ms. Watson stared down Wendy and blocked every possible attempt to respond to or appeal this abrupt decision.

Wendy's smile switched to tight and trembling lips. This was absolutely unfair. She tried to keep her eyes focused on Ms. Watson's, but after a few seconds a tear popped out of her left eye and started a slow path down her cheek. Wendy turned around and left.

Sometimes You Need to Let Go

Noah spent his holidays in Bayfield. He wanted to stay away from his house; there were too many memories, too many shattered dreams.

At Bayfield, his initiatives were thriving, and he felt more at home walking on those streets than in his house. He was starting to doubt what his real life was…

The holidays ended, and he had to return to work. He remembered the high-profile case coming up and wondered if it was going to be the same one.

He also remembered that Joshua had quit right after he learned he would not be participating on the case.

Noah felt he had no energy left. He could not deal with the pressure of the press, Wendy's mood swings, the promotion, and all that this case entailed. It was exhausting the first time, and he was not looking forward to living through it again.

The first day back at work, Noah headed to Ms. Watson's office and presented his resignation. That would allow Wendy and Joshua to work on the case coming up. Ms. Watson refused to accept Noah's resignation at first, but Noah was very convincing and stubborn about it.

He had a big smile after saying goodbye to all the team, and he headed to the door for the last time. Then he fainted again. He just plummeted to the floor. As usual, all went black, and in a few seconds he was watching his body in the hospital bed.

It was different this time. Madelyn was holding his hand. "I love you, Daddy," she said, and kissed his forehead. The nurse walked her out.

Grace was wearing all black. She looked really sad. She grabbed his hand and pressed it against her chest. She kissed him on the lips and told the doctor, "It's time."

"Are you sure, Grace? Everything is paid until the end of this month. There is no need to do it now."

"Please be sure to return the money to whoever sent it. I have made up my mind. Please proceed."

The doctor and the nurse started to disconnect the respirator and all the tubes in Noah's body. Soon the beeping of his heart was the only sound in the room. The frequency started decreasing. It was almost as if you could see life slowly draining away from his body.

Grace's eyes were full of tears and her hands were holding Noah's tightly, as though she wanted to keep his life from leaving his body.

It was hard to tell if time was passing at all. There was no weight, no pain. He could not hear Grace any more...but everything stopped. He did have a sensation of completeness and happiness. He had Grace holding his hand through this passage.

When Am I?

So now what? He didn't see the tunnel this time. The mysterious voice that gave him his marching orders was mute now. He didn't hear or feel Grace anymore.

"Daddy, Daddy!" Noah was excited to hear Madelyn's voice, but couldn't see anything. "I am falling," Madelyn said, and all of a sudden Noah felt a knock on his head. It hurt—but he was feeling something. It was the ground; it was cold. He also felt Madelyn's feet kicking his head.

Slowly he was able to open his eyes. It took him a few seconds to realize where he was. It was his front yard. The air smelled like spring.

Madelyn was on top of him. She had just fallen off the branch of a tree right over his head and knocked him to the ground.

"Are you OK, Daddy?"

"Yes, sweetie, how are you?"

"I'm OK."

Then, like unexpected thunder, Grace's voice came from within the house. "Are you guys OK?"

"Yes, Mom, I fell out of the tree, and Dad tried to catch me, but he couldn't," Madelyn responded, giggling.

Noah stood up and ran toward Grace. He hugged her; he hugged her hard. He had been wishing to do that for so long.

Madelyn laughed. "I think I scared him!" She kept giggling.

"What's happening?" Grace asked, surprised by Noah's hug.

"Not sure," Noah responded, "but I just want to hug you."

The hug was interrupted by a phone call. Noah picked up the phone, unsure of...well, basically everything at this point.

"Hello?"

"Is this Mr. Noah Blakely?"

"Yes, speaking."

"Good morning, I hope this is a good time."

"Who is this?"

"This is Mr. Joshua Swartsman from Watson & Corcoran. We interviewed you last week, and we are very impressed by your credentials. If you are still interested in joining our firm, I will be mailing you an offer today."

"Joshua?"

"Yes, we interviewed last week. I hope you are still interested."

It was Joshua's voice. It sounded distant and formal, as if they didn't really know each other. Noah didn't know what was going on.

"Sure, thanks," Noah responded. "Please mail it to me. I will be glad to review it."

"OK, please feel free to contact me should you have any questions."

"Will do, thanks."

"Who was it?" Grace asked, curiously.

"It was from Watson & Corcoran. They are offering me a position there, Noah responded, still feeling lost.

"Isn't that the job that you wanted?"

"I thought it was, but I am confused now."

"Do you think you have a concussion? I mean, Madelyn fell right on your head."

"Nothing serious, just a bit shocked," Noah said.

"Did I hurt you, Daddy?"

"Not at all, sweetie. Let's get your bike out and go for a ride."

"What bike?" Madelyn asked.

And that's when Noah realized. He had woken up before taking the job. He had a chance now to choose a new life, to make better decisions than the ones he had just lived through.

"Well, let's go and get you one."

Madelyn's smile illuminated the house.

"I will have to hit you in the head more often," Grace joked.

Noah sighed while looking at Grace. A smile appeared on his face. He looked at her with admiration and realized he had in her and Madelyn everything he could possibly need to be the happiest person in the world.

He responded: "You make life worth living, even if it's more than once."